The Road to Sugar Loaf
A Suffragist's Story

The Road to Sugar Loaf

A Suffragist's Story

A Novel

Eric T. Reynolds

HADLEY
RILLE
BOOKS

Cover Design © Hadley Rille Books
Cover Photography:
Sugar Loaf Hill, Greenwood Co, KS © Sherry Stapleford
Author Photo © Nancy Reynolds

ISBN-13 978-1-7350938-2-6

Trade Paperback Edition

Other editions Available:
Hardcover
Ebook
Audiobook

Edited by Laura Ripper and Rose Reynolds
v2.2
Published in the United States of America, and worldwide by
Hadley Rille Books
Kansas City, USA
www.hrbpress.com
contact@hadleyrillebooks.com

To the memory of Ruth Wiebel (Nana)
who at age 30 could finally vote

Acknowledgments

I appreciate the assistance and encouragement of others when writing this novel including from my first readers Sherry Stapleford, Debi Carbaugh Robinson, and Nancy Reynolds.

I found valuable information from: the Kansas Historical Society site, the book, *Jailed for Freedom: American Women Win the Vote* by Doris Stevens (pub. 1920), the National Women's Party site, the archives of the *Topeka Capital-Journal* newspaper, National Weather Services, and the Congressional Record, and other sites. Plus, I thank Dr. Kathy Pierron Chartrand for historical advice on early twentieth century medicine. And also good advice from conversations with Diana Carlin Pierron, Rose and Nancy Reynolds, and my first readers, Sherry and Debi.

Introduction

Once upon a time, a hundred years ago, U.S. Secretary of State Bainbridge Colby signed the proclamation at 8:00AM on August 26, 1920, that certified ratification of the Nineteenth Amendment granting women the right to vote after an almost century-long Suffrage struggle by thousands of women and men.

This is the story of an American woman from the Midwest and several colleagues who joined the struggle in the last decade that led to passage of the Amendment. This novel shows their involvement and challenges within the local, statewide and national Suffrage Movement.

This is a work of fiction, but I tried to adhere to historical facts as much as possible and any literary license taken with some events is only my interpretation. Many women and some men endured violence and harassment in the Suffrage Movement. The story includes a little of that based on published firsthand accounts by suffragists of actual events; some scenes were difficult to write, not for lack of information but for having to experience reliving some of the brutality they endured. Referring to the Movement as a struggle is an enormous understatement.

The sacrifices of the Suffragists should never be forgotten. The main character and her friends and acquaintances are purely fictional as is her town. She does meet several suffragists from history in her journey. As I strive to portray an accurate historical story, any errors not caught by my editors are my own.

—Eric T. Reynolds, August 2020

It is better, as far as getting the vote is concerned I believe, to have a small, united group than an immense debating society.

—Alice Paul, American Suffragist

PROLOGUE

Spring 1894

The Flint Hills Outside Sycamore Falls, Kansas

Kathryn Wolfe vaulted over the boulder. An outcrop loomed above. This was the fastest she'd ever made it this far.

"Trailing and climbing on rocks is no place for a lady," she had heard too many times.

She loved the exertion of trailing up hills—and if boulders got in the way all the better—but as she reached up for a handhold on the craggy ledge and was about to call up to her friend Mary, she gave in to the temptation to glance out at the sea of green hills rippling to the horizon.

She shouldn't have. At least the grassy area a little ways down was free of rocks.

The Road to Sugar Loaf: A Suffragist's Story

This was Kathryn's second attempt to scale that rocky protrusion. And on its second attempt, Suffrage failed to pass in Kansas that year.

CHAPTER ONE

September 1911

Sycamore Falls High School

During the fourth week of school, lockers and the lingering scent of freshly painted walls greeted civics teacher George Fielding as he walked the long, echoing hallway. He stopped outside Principal Holt's office when Violette emerged and handed him a string-clasped envelope. He peeked inside to find Suffrage leaflets and other printed materials.

Violette looked around the hallway. "It arrived today from The Kansas Equal Suffrage Association," she whispered.

He thanked her and continued to his classroom where several students stood laughing next to the open door. They looked away when he approached. Upon entering the classroom, some students tried to suppress their snickering. Their glances toward the blackboard revealed what amused them.

George saw a caricature of himself wearing a dress while holding a sign that said, "Women Vote."

He smiled and turned to the class. "I see some of you are interested in Women's Suffrage, and I commend the artist for making me more handsome than I actually am, but that dress should persuade you not to pursue a career in fashion design."

Jesse Gaines raised his hand. "Mr. Fielding, does that mean we're not in trouble?"

"Do you think you should be in trouble, Mr. Gaines?"

Jesse sank down in his chair and shook his head.

George stepped beneath the portrait of Lincoln next to the blackboard and held up a stack of printed material. "Mr. Gaines's artwork is timely," he said. "Since the Women's Suffrage referendum was passed in February, it will be on the ballot in next year's election. I am authorized to invite all of you to write an essay for the county contest about why Kansans should vote for Women's Suffrage. The essay is voluntary, but I will offer extra credit for anyone who participates, something that should help your grade, Mr. Gaines."

Laughter.

"All right, everyone, Mr. Gaines isn't the only student here who can use extra credit." George held up the papers again. "Come by my desk after class and take notes from this material for good information on Women's Suffrage."

CHAPTER TWO

May 1912

The Flint Hills West of Sycamore Falls, Kansas

Kathryn steered Annabelle over the rough terrain on the grassy hillside and pulled her up to a stop when they approached the top of the hill. On this warm day in May, there was nothing like the feeling of wind through one's hair while taking in the commanding view from up here on horseback, the rooftops of Sycamore Falls in the valley, the sea of green prairie hills all around. Mary caught up to her, and then urged her horse to a gallop. Kathryn took the challenge, dismissing that little voice in her head that said no.

* * *

She didn't think anything was broken and her impaired leg felt all right. She decided to lie still and not try to get up in a panic. Annabelle stood nearby and snorted an apology while shaking her head up and down, even though the spill wasn't the horse's fault. Mary stood over Kathryn, her silhouette blocking the blazing noonday sun.

Kathryn sat up and brushed off her riding clothes. Her hat sat in the grass a few feet away and she put it back on after Mary fetched it.

"Don't move, Kathryn," Mary said as she knelt next to her. "Let me check you over."

Kathryn caught her breath. "Now you can practice your nursing training."

"I'm not a nurse yet. Lie still and keep quiet. How do your legs feel? Especially the left leg? I'm sorry, but I thought we could talk up here away from curious ears."

Mary gently examined Kathryn's neck, arms, legs, and pelvis, and asked if she had pain in various locations. Kathryn didn't think she was really hurt, just the potential for a bruise or two.

The shade under a nearby tree looked inviting.

Kathryn stood to take Annabelle's reins and led her to the lone tree just up the hill, the tree she should have steered Annabelle safely around before the horse banked and threw her. She wasn't an experienced rider, especially on a galloping horse over a hillside strewn with rocks. She tied the reins to a sturdy branch. Mary led her horse to the tree and secured it to the branch.

A breeze flowed up there and it was cool beneath the foliage.

To the west was another grassy hill. A farmhouse with wraparound porch stood near its top.

"There's Ida's place," Kathryn said.

Mary gazed over. "We should pay her a visit. It's been a while."

"Maybe she would consider starting up the book club again."

"I would like that," said Mary. "I've also heard she wants to form a Women's Club."

Kathryn eyed a spot under the tree where she could sit back against the tree trunk and take in this birdseye view of Sycamore Falls and the scenery.

"Kathryn, no!"

Just as she was about to sit she saw it.

"At least it's not poisonous," said Mary.

A four-foot-long black snake slithered up the trunk toward the foliage. The horses were getting restless, so Mary led them from the tree.

A man on horse trotting around the base of the hill waved up to them.

"Oh, good," Mary said. "There's Pa. Let's go down and have lunch. Can you ride?"

Kathryn laughed. "Apparently not very well."

"Just takes practice. Annabelle's a gentle mare, but she's quick and agile. Let's go." She helped Kathryn clamber up to the saddle. Annabelle was calm now; Kathryn settled onto her and they rode down to the Dodd's big house. The hilltop breeze faded as they descended.

"I can come over Tuesday evening," Mary said just before they reached the shaded backyard.

"Sounds lovely," said Kathryn. "I won't mention anything at lunch."

"Pa doesn't know what we're up to; he'll probably think we'll be discussing bookshop business. It's best to keep talk of the gathering to ourselves."

* * *

Later that day, Kathryn returned home and opened the windows to let in the breeze. The house was about ten years old and the warmth of the day had brought out the scent of the somewhat recently applied shellac finish on the woodwork's dark stain.

That evening, she puttered around the house. Her bruises were too achy to do anything but sit in the living room and read, so she lit the kerosene lamp on the little table next to her reading chair. She didn't have fancy gas or electric lights in her house yet. Perhaps in a couple of years. Lighting the rooms like this was one of the old-fashioned traditions she found acceptable. She settled into the chair and cracked open *Molly Make Believe* by Eleanor Hallowell Abbott, her most recent acquisition.

But it had been a tiring day and rather than fall asleep here while reading, she went up to bed.

CHAPTER THREE

May 1912

Main Street Bookshop

Kathryn opened Main Street Bookshop mid-morning the next day as she always did, balancing on her cane as she stepped over the threshold. After settling in to her first task, in walked someone she hadn't seen for years. She was about Kathryn's age, looking fashionable in the new decade style.

"You must be Kathryn," she said.

Kathryn was setting up a new book display with *Moving the Mountain* by Charlotte Perkins Gilman. After she finished arranging the table, she turned to greet her visitor.

"I'm sorry," she said, "I wanted to set this up before more customers arrive."

"Do you remember me?" the woman asked.

"Of course I do. You're Anna, aren't you?"

Anna smiled and glanced around the shop. "I was in Ida's Book Club with you. Do you remember we met there a while back?"

"Yes, of course! Where have you taken yourself to?"

"I married two years after leaving the club and we moved to Topeka. He left me for someone else and I recently decided Sycamore Falls was the best place for me now."

"I'm glad you're back in Sycamore Falls." Kathryn hadn't liked Anna back during their book club days, but was happy she was getting on with her life. Perhaps they could reconcile their differences.

Anna sighed. "Me, too. I missed it here."

The door's little bell jingled, and Mary stepped in.

"We got the new books in?" Mary said.

She turned to Anna. "Well, hello, I heard you were back recently. Glad to see you." Mary leaned toward her. "I love the silver leaf design of your earrings."

"Thank you," Anna said. She stepped away toward an alcove along a wall. "I'd like to browse around a little."

"Yes, of course," said Mary.

Anna smiled, went to one of the curved wooden library steps in the alcove, climbed it, selected a book from a high shelf and flipped through it.

Kathryn peered over at Anna for a moment.

Just as the door's little bell jingled again, Anna put the book back and stepped off the small ladder.

"Thank you," she said to Mary and Kathryn, brushing past the man who entered as she left the bookshop.

The man exchanged greetings with Kathryn and Mary and went to look at some of the new fiction titles.

Mary took that opportunity to lean toward Kathryn and whisper, "Anna's coming to the meeting tonight."

"Ah," Kathryn said, "that's why she was browsing the women's 'subversive' titles."

"She came by one afternoon last week when I was tending shop alone and wanted to talk about Women's Suffrage," Mary said.

Kathryn didn't seem surprised, picked up one of the new copies of *Women's Suffrage: A Short History of a Great Movement,* and thumbed through it.

The man left and another man entered.

"Why, Mr. Fielding," Mary said.

"Good morning, ladies," he said. "It's been a while, hasn't it?" He looked at the book display. "I see you've received that book. I should like to purchase one."

"Yes, of course," said Mary, stepping around to the back of the counter.

"Is this a story that will interest you?" Kathryn asked him.

"Any story with a different point of view told in an entertaining way interests me."

"That's commendable," Kathryn said.

Mary gave her a look indicating Kathryn's manner of speech was curious. Kathryn knew she embarrassed her sometimes.

Mr. Fielding bought his book and left the shop. Mary followed him out, returning soon after.

"He's a nice man," Kathryn said. "He would be welcome to come to the meeting tonight."

"He is going to attend," said Mary. "I just invited him."

Mary started to set up a table in the women's section alcove while Kathryn finished arranging the display of new books.

"It'd be nice to have meetings there," Kathryn said, pointing to the alcove, "but it's probably best at my home so people won't notice a gathering of women here and start asking questions."

"I'm fixing this alcove so customers can relax here," Mary said.

The door jingled and Fred Markley from Markley's Furniture Company a couple of doors down entered the shop. The scent of cigar smoke imbedded in his clothes came in with him. He was around fifty with a characteristic full beard laced with gray.

"Hello there," he said in his gravelly voice. "Mrs. Markley asked me to pick up a book for her." He reached for a copy of *Women's Suffrage: A Short History of a Great Movement.* "This is the one, I believe."

Kathryn went to the counter. "Say, Mr. Markley, I notice you have a new selection of wicker furniture."

"We do indeed. Any style you want."

"I'd love to come over and browse, but Mary and I are quite busy during the day."

He reached into his pocket and produced a key. "Then go take a look yourself when it's convenient." He handed the key to her and placed the book onto the counter with a silver dollar. "I'll take this one."

They settled up and he stashed the book into his jacket and left.

* * *

Later that day, Kathryn went into the furniture store and the late afternoon sun spilled into the dim, cavernous room that was filled with wicker furniture of all kinds. A door halfway back on the right led to another room she couldn't see into. In here, round tables with chairs filled this room. She had an eerie feeling, as if dozens of people were sitting all around the room not allowed to make their presence known. A table in the shadowy back caught her attention. She had goosebumps as she meandered back to it, sliding between the furniture displays. The wicker table with slightly mismatched chairs appealed to her sense of style. Perhaps they would go well on her porch. She noticed the door to the darker adjoining room again and went over to peer in. Dark, wooden furniture throughout the large room exaggerated the gloom. In the middle of the room was a secretary desk with the lid folded out. It held a couple of paper sheets. She went to the desk and squinted to see what was written on them. One was a letter, the other, an invitation of some kind.

The letter began—

Dear Mr. Markley:

You are, no doubt, aware of the growing woman suffrage movement, both in Kansas and nationwide. As a businessman, you surely know the risk to the national economy should woman suffrage eventually become law.

A new group is forming. As you are a well-respected man in our community, we would invite you. . .

A gravelly voice startled her. "The best wicker pieces are in the other room." Fred Markley's silhouette stood in the doorway.

She suppressed a gasp. "Oh, yes, I found a table with two chairs I like. I also wanted to look at the desks in here."

"Very well," he said with a smile. "Come show me the table and chairs."

She followed him into the wicker room to show him. She could spend more time looking, but that letter reminded her she needed to get home to prepare for a meeting.

CHAPTER FOUR

May 1912

Event Planning

Mary sat on the sofa in Kathryn's living room while Kathryn fetched her a cup of tea.

"I think we should welcome everyone who wants to get involved," Mary said when Kathryn returned to the living room.

"You're right, of course."

"Anna is bringing a gentleman friend she says is friendly to Women's Suffrage."

"The more men friendly to Suffrage, the better," Kathryn said. "How does she know him?"

"I think they're courting. I've seen him around town, but he's usually alone or with business associates, I think."

"Well then, if they are, I'm glad she might have someone special after that break up with her husband in Topeka."

"Yes, he's quite wealthy, I think."

"That's wonderful," Kathryn said.

She went to the rolltop desk along the wall and retrieved a piece of paper with some notes and handed it to Mary.

Mary studied it and said, "This will do nicely. Do you think we can get Memorial Hall for an event like this?"

"I spoke to Christine at the city clerk's office. She said it's available for any kind of meeting we want to plan. In fact, I think she might want to attend."

A knock at the door interrupted them. Kathryn went to answer it, greeted Anna and a man with her.

She took them into the living room where Anna and Mary exchanged pleasantries. Anna introduced her friend, John Shane.

"It's nice to have gentlemen join us, Mr. Shane," said Mary.

"My pleasure," he said.

"You won't be alone, Mr. Shane," Kathryn said, "George Fielding will join us, too."

"Ah yes," he said. "The school teacher."

More women arrived: Florence, Sarah, and Alice. George Fielding arrived soon after and took a seat next to John Shane. With everyone seated, Kathryn passed the sheet around with her notes about planning the event. Most expressed agreement. John and George both nodded as well.

"Let's not disclose around town our organizing of this until after the event," Kathryn said.

Everyone mumbled in agreement.

Kathryn sat at her small desk with pencil ready to take notes as they planned the event, getting a speaker, and publicizing it. With two men present, the conversation inevitably came around to how and why they became interested in Women's Suffrage.

"If I may," said George. John nodded; he had no objection, so George began:

"It occurred to me during one of my jaunts in the woods as ideas often manifest themselves there. On an autumn day in 1909, when I was out cataloging the various kinds of trees one encounters in the wooded valleys around here, I trailed downhill through chest-high grass and reached the woods, where I started noting the oaks and sycamores that towered over me. As fall was getting on, I had a colorful canopy of foliage overhead. I stepped into the woods and meandered around the tall trees, kicking through piles of fallen leaves. I followed what was perhaps an old buffalo trail deep in the woods and came upon one of those stone fences that comes up to my waist.

"You, no doubt, have noticed I walk with a limp, a childhood injury. My bad leg didn't allow me to climb over the rock fence—you can relate to that, Kathryn, if I may— so I walked along the fence to see what boundary it marked. After a bit of a walk, I came to a corner. The rock fence was rectangular for I could see to the next corner on my left. I noticed something within the fenced area and walked around the corner to get a better look. When I reached a break in the trees, I saw the ruins of an old stone house, one of the abandoned homesteads around the area. This one was probably a few decades old, and some of the window cross timbers were charred, so it appeared the house had to be abandoned. I wanted to get close to the old structure, but I couldn't scale that little wall no matter how hard I tried. The ruined house wasn't just a curiosity for me. I wanted to examine it as a subject for class discussion about the Homestead Act. I even thought about taking my students there.

"And then I realized I was prevented from reaching the ruin simply because of a physical characteristic of my leg. 'What,' I thought, 'if someone who is informed and intelligent is prevented from participating in our great democracy simply because of her gender?'

"I knew then that women deserved the right to vote and one's sex shouldn't preclude her from voting."

"That's an interesting account, Mr. Fielding," said John. "I admit it is taking me a while to accept the merits of Woman Suffrage, but I'm coming around."

"I commend you for your open-mindedness," said Kathryn.

John appeared he would have tipped his hat at Kathryn had he been wearing one.

Anna stood. "I apologize I can't stay longer, but I must go." She turned to John. "Mr. Shane, may I ask for a ride home?"

"He flashed her a warm smile, nodded, and Anna went to the porch to wait.

The others mentioned their appreciation to Kathryn and got ready to leave. Mary lingered as Kathryn acknowledged the others leaving. John Shane stood and a calling card fell out of his jacket pocket onto the chair. Kathryn almost said something, but she still had other guests to bid farewell.

Mary stayed until John left.

"I think they *are* courting," Mary whispered. "Anna and Mr. Shane."

"I think so, too," Kathryn said. "And they're not public about it."

"But why not?"

"Who knows? You never know with her," Kathryn said with a chuckle.

"She hasn't changed."

* * *

Kathryn's housekeeper, Martha, came by Kathryn's house midday Friday.

"Well, Miss Wolfe," she said, starting to straighten the doilies on the sofa back. I'm seeing those posters up all over town about the big meeting at Memorial Hall. If I may be so bold to ask, are you planning to attend? What I mean is, if you can see to allow it, I'd like to take that day off and attend, myself."

"Of course, Martha, I won't need you that day. It's an important meeting all of us women should attend. I'll be there, too."

A few minutes later, Martha stood next to one of the living room chairs and held up a calling card she found stuck in the cushion.

She handed it to Kathryn. On the blank side, written in hurried handwriting was: *Contact Mr. Theodore Miller, 210 North Main Street, Sycamore Falls regarding preliminary meeting.*

Kathryn flipped the card over and it had in fancy printed script: "John Shane, Investment Advisor."
"I'll give this to Anna and she can give it back to Mr. Shane," Martha said.

"Thank you. Will you see her?"

"We live in the same boarding house."

* * *

The next Wednesday, John Shane arrived at Theodore Miller's office on North Main Street just after midday and stepped through the door. Theodore Miller emerged from a back office.

"John, how do you do?" Miller said, extending his hand.

John took it and said. "I've been busy."

"No doubt you have with the ways of the economy these past couple of years. That Sherman Antitrust Act has a lot of people on edge, especially men of business. You must be doing well with stock sell orders. I may ask for your services should I decide it's time to trade."

John smiled and nodded.

"But I had another reason for asking you here," Miller said.

"Mrs. Miller can't find a way to mend an unmentionable. She is looking for someone who does garment mending at home. Do you know of a lady who does this kind of work? It's a complete mystery to me."

John managed a small smile. "It's a mystery to me, too. If Mrs. Miller calls on my acquaintance, we can clear up that mystery."

Miller set a small box secured with string onto the desk in front of John. "Mrs. Miller will call on her." Miller sat back to end that discussion.

"Now then," Miller continued. "The National Association Opposed to Woman Suffrage. I want to talk about that. I'm getting involved with it."

"I see," said John.

Miller tapped his index finger on the box. "But you support the effort opposing Suffrage?"

John sat up. "Oh, yes."

"Then I think the upcoming meeting with businessmen like us will help us build the local chapter, don't you?"

"No doubt it will."

Miller sat forward and leaned over the box. "Well then, my boy, I thank you for coming by, and as I said Mrs. Miller will call on your acquaintance."

"I'll let her know."

The Road to Sugar Loaf: A Suffragist's Story

CHAPTER FIVE

May 1912

The Hill

By Saturday, it had been three weeks since the last rain drenched the area, and George Fielding scarcely had need to watch for mud as he hiked along the country road. This was one of those canopy roads somewhat common in the Flint Hills. Plenty of shade kept things cool here, but the foliage obscured his view of the hill. No matter, he knew his destination was ahead and the break in the wooden pole fence that lined the road was just ahead and led to the trail.

A man of about fifty emerged from there on horseback. George continued walking and the man rode up to him.

"Good day to you," the man said.

George returned the greeting and nodded toward the trail entrance.

Fred Markley smiled and that meant George could go ahead through Markley's land.

George entered the woods and headed along the trail, trudging through the woods over rocky terrain, and after half an hour, he emerged into the sun and onto tallgrass prairie. He walked up a gentle but rocky rise. Up there, he saw a mostly wooded valley ahead with a clearing where the ramparts of Sugar Loaf began. The discarded wood and metal debris in the clearing he had noticed on previous hikes caught his attention. He decided to take a look this time and went down toward it. Not until he reached the area could he peer through the tallgrass and tell what it was: an old covered wagon in ruins resting at an angle, missing its cover with a couple of the support bows still intact but missing the yoke with the lower half of the assembly covered by the sediments of time.

The hilltop was a ways up and he looked forward to the shaded Promontory with a view halfway up, his favorite stopping place on the hill. He followed the old buffalo-beaten path up.

By the time he reached the Promontory, the breeze picked up, sending waves rolling along the grassy hillsides. The shade under the grove of trees was refreshing. He retrieved a canteen, quenched his thirst, and sat to take in the view across the rolling green hills. This was a great place to relax and think.

He gazed down at the remnants of the broken down covered wagon, perhaps belonging to a homesteader. George imagined their struggle. He thought more about the peoples whose land was taken, the subject of some of his class lessons.

He sighed and sat back on his elbows not sure what to think. A stone poked him, sending him sitting up again: the ring of stones of an old campfire. He hadn't noticed it before.

Markley was generous to let George hike up here whenever he liked. "But we need to talk if I decide to graze cattle there," Markley had said.

A glance at his pocket watch indicated moving on if he was going to reach the top today.

Sugar Loaf wasn't steep on this side, but his old injury made it difficult clambering up the rocks that ringed the hill just below the hilltop. On the summit, he held his hat against the wind and felt the roar of the breezes across his ears. A quick scan of the surrounding lowland allowed him to take inventory of the trees that he recorded on a folded ledger sheet. They were mostly near the creek that meandered through the valley. Oak, hickory, cottonwood, interspersed with towering sycamores.

The climb as always was worth the challenge. He looked around at the Flint Hills panorama.

"Ad Astra per Aspera," he said aloud, reciting the Kansas state motto. "To the stars through difficulties. Some goals are worth overcoming the challenges. This hill and something else."

He sighed and prepared to head down the hill.

Meanwhile

Ida greeted Kathryn on the porch of her hilltop house, inviting her to sit where the view was best. It was nice to relax up here after a busy week at the bookshop. She settled onto the wicker chair and accepted a glass of tea. The lilacs were blooming, filling the air with their sweet aroma.

From here, she could gaze at the sunlit panorama to the southwest. A distinctively-shaped hill rose from surrounding hills on the horizon.

"Thank you," Kathryn said, taking a sip of tea. "Those rolling hills are beautiful—say, you have a great view of Sugar Loaf from here." She pointed to the prominent hill. Barren of cattle, it had a small trail she could just make out near its base from where it went up slope.

"Yes we do. It's one of the reasons we chose this house," Ida said.

Kathryn focused on the path and imagined trailing along it, but it looked quite inaccessible for her nowadays.

"I should like to climb it," Kathryn said.

"I think you could manage it," Ida said. "George Fielding trails in the hills often, including that one. Perhaps he can take you."

"That would be wonderful. I'll ask him when convenient."

Ida took a seat next to her. "Margarete will be by soon," she said.

"How wonderful. I haven't seen her in ages. I think Mary is on her way as well."

Mary pulled up in horse and buggy followed by Margarete on horseback.

They secured their horses next to Ida's water trough and came up to the porch.

Kathryn stood. "Thank you for tending shop this afternoon," she said to Mary.

Mary smiled and extended her hands toward her. "Yes and now that we're here, I know you want to talk about the hills."

"Do I go on about them?" Kathryn asked.

Mary suppressed a giggle. "On and on and on."

"Well then, I won't refrain from it if you can tolerate that."

"Not at all, dear Kathryn." Mary accepted a glass of tea and they sat.

They dropped the small talk so Margarete and Kathryn could catch up.

"It's normal to miss the hills," Margaret said to Kathryn.

"Well," Margarete said proudly, "I have a bit of news."

"Oh?" said Ida.

"You go ahead first, Mary and Kathryn," Margarete said. "What about the hills?"

"Kathryn's been talking about getting out in nature for weeks with the nicer weather now," Mary said.

"Yes," Kathryn said, pointing at Sugar Loaf. "I'd love to climb that hill when I'm able."

"Perhaps Mr. Fielding will take you on a hike there or even several of us ladies," said Mary. "You remember George. Fielding, don't you, Margarete?"

"I certainly do. Quite the nature lover, as I remember. It seems Kathryn has found a way into his heart."

"No, he's a good friend. I'll welcome him taking us trailing."

"All I know about it," Mary said, "is Mr. Markley owns it and the surrounding land, and George says you can see half the county from up there."

Kathryn couldn't contain her excitement.

"He must take us with you," Margarete said. "Prepare a picnic lunch. It'll be wonderful."

"Keep your sights set on it, Kathryn," Mary said. "We'll get there, perhaps soon."

"I'm ready!" Kathryn said. "What is your news, Margarete?"

"Well, there's a Women's Suffrage parade planned for next March in Washington, DC, and I think we should go, don't you, Kathryn? I want to plan a trip."

"I've been thinking about it," said Kathryn. "I'm already putting money aside."

The Road to Sugar Loaf: A Suffragist's Story

"Then this is a good time to tell you all," Ida said. "With Women's Suffrage picking up, I will form a Women's Club and will affiliate it with the National Federation of Women's Clubs. I plan to invite the past members of our book club to join. Let's keep this between us here until it's established."

CHAPTER SIX

June 1912

Judgmental

Theodore Miller, Fred Markley, and John Shane stood on the corner outside Ranchers Bank downtown one morning.

"Well, Shane," said Miller, "in keeping with our chance meeting here in front of the bank, are you still keeping banker hours?"

"I won't pretend to match your knack for the same, Mr. Miller."

"Then I will avoid overdoing. Will you do the same?"

Mayor MacGregor walked up. "Say, gentlemen, don't you know loitering is illegal?"

"Speaking of banker hours," Markley said. "You won't get reelected with the hours you keep, MacGregor!"

Miller pointed down Main Street. "About banker hours, there's that bookshop keeper with the cockeyed leg opening her store at this time like always. Now there's someone who'll never vote for you, or vote for anybody at all."

"She's only kind of a looker with that funny walk," MacGregor said.

"She fell off a ledge up above our ranch a few years ago," Miller said.

"What do you know about her, Shane? Is she courting?"

"What do you think, with that bum leg? I don't really know much about her. I've heard you don't cross her, because she's got a mouth on her that'll knock you down faster than a ranch hand's."

"Well, I haven't heard that," Markley said, "and I was a ranch hand in my youth, so I won't test her."

"What about her possibly courting that school teacher?" Miller said. "Or maybe that co-owner of the shop would be better suited for her."

"There are plenty of reasons to avoid her, I'm sure," Shane said, "not to mention she's one of those Suffragettes."

Miller gestured a block north to the courthouse. "She might end up in there someday."

MacGregor puffed out his chest. "She could live to regret it if she makes trouble. I don't need any changes happening in my town."

"We should keep an eye on both women who run that shop," Miller said.

"And George Fielding," Shane said.

"He's harmless," MacGregor said.

Miller looked toward the hotel and gestured toward it. "Do you see who I see? Do you know who that is? None other than Jane Addams."

"Who's Jane Addams?" MacGregor asked.

"Somebody who can stir up more trouble than you'll want," Miller said. "She's here to speak at that Suffrage event at Memorial Hall."

"Let her speak for all the good it'll do them," MacGregor said.

* * *

Pop finished trimming George Fielding's hair.

"There," Pop said, "that should do you. How are your teeth?"

"George laughed and pulled his right cheek to the side. "I think I've got a molar back here that needs to come out."

Pop chuckled. "Not for a hundred years has that happened in this barber shop."

Lou and Richard, waiting for a cut, snickered.

"And if they did," Lou said, "you couldn't trust ol' Pop here to yank out the right one!"

Pop sneered. "All right, Lou, your haircut will cost one cent extra."

"I vote for that," Richard said.

"I second it," said George. "And speaking of voting, are we really afraid that women voting will cause broken homes and men will no longer have wives?"

The others grumbled.

"Many women don't even want the vote and their votes would cancel out their husbands' anyway," Richard said.

"Do they need it?" Lou asked.

"Say, Fielding," said Pop, "what's in it for you?"

George straightened up. "Fairness," he said as he stood.

"Bah," replied Pop. "They should be happy with the role they have now."

"Ask yourself, Pop, would you be?" insisted George.

Pop scoffed at the suggestion. "Yep. I would if I was a woman which I ain't, but I don't think you should come in here anymore."

"Time for me to go and get away from this sap," Lou said.

"Go on, Fielding," Pop said, "no charge. I ain't doing business with no male Suffragette."

"Yeah," Lou said, "what happens if you get your way? They get the vote, the economy sinks and ol' Pop here's out of business."

"The governor, chief justice of the Supreme Court, and others support the men's pro-Suffrage organization," George mumbled.

"I didn't vote for Stubbs anyway," Pop said.

"Come on, you traitor," Lou said as he waved George out the door.

As they stepped onto the sidewalk, Pop stuck his head out, and shouted, "Fielding! I don't want you in here again!"

Lou and Richard roared with laughter, slapping each other's back.

CHAPTER SEVEN

June 1912

Trailing Hopes

The timeless smell of old books greeted Kathryn when she stepped into the Sycamore Falls Library. Established in 1880, it began operations five years after the Blue Rapids Public Library, the first library in Kansas.

Florence was the librarian here now, and she took Kathryn through the long aisle to a back room that had a large table with a map spread across the top. George Fielding was there poring over the map. He looked up and smiled. "Hello, Kathryn. There's a rumor going around that you would like to trail Sugar Loaf."

"Rumor, no. Are you implying you'll take us up there?"

"I am excited to show you all the wonders of it." He smoothed the map and traced his finger over it. "Here is where West Hill Road goes through these trees. From there, we can access the trail here." He pointed at the location.

"I'll arrange with you all for next Saturday if that's agreeable."

"Oh, yes. Do you need to ask Mr. Markley for permission?"

"Not at all. We're welcome to enjoy it."

* * *

A week later, George led Mary and Kathryn along the road toward the opening in the fence.

"It's too bad Anna couldn't join us," said Mary. "She said she's meeting Mr. Shane. Do you think it's about investment advice?"

"What do you think?" Kathryn said.

Mary held a hand to her mouth.

As George was about to speak, a car headed toward them then stopped in front of the break in the fence.

Markley stepped from the car and faced them. "I'm afraid the trail is off limits now," he said.

George frowned in disbelief. "Off limits, sir?"

"I'm afraid so. Stepping through the fence amounts to trespassing. You have a right to this road, but you may as well turn back and go home. That trail is too treacherous for the lady anyway."

"Is there another way?" Kathryn asked, ignoring that comment.

Markley didn't answer.

George offered his elbows to Mary and Kathryn and they turned to head back the way they came.

Mary and Kathryn tried to hold their heads up. Their chance to go up Sugar Loaf and they hit a dead end.

Kathryn kicked a dirt clod; it tumbled ahead. "How is it he just now forbids access?" she asked. "I've walked a lot on this leg, so the hike *shouldn't* be treacherous for me. We won't know until we try."

They continued on.

"We'll keep working toward the eventual success of the Suffrage Movement," George said, changing the subject.

They reached a curve in the road. There was a clearing ahead where sunlight lit the road.

"If we work hard, we might achieve Suffrage," Mary said. "But I'm not expecting anything great to happen."

When they reached the clearing, they saw grassland on the right.

George stopped, adjusted his hat, and went to lean over the fence.

"There's been progress," he said. "A new open-mindedness in this century after the 1894 Kansas Suffrage vote failed."

They went on beyond the grassland and Sugar Loaf dominated the landscape.

As they stopped to look, Mary said, "It's so close. Will we ever get up there?"

"We will!" Kathryn said. "You said yourself to keep sights set on it. We just need to keep trying."

George retrieved a couple of folded newspaper articles from a pocket. "I brought these to show you all. I planned to show them to you when we reached the hilltop. Governor Stubbs is friendly toward Suffrage." George held out clippings from *The Sycamore Falls Weekly Prospect*."

He passed the clippings around. Kathryn read them and then gazed out over the prairie at Sugar Loaf. She could almost reach across and touch it.

"You know Mr. Markley," Mary said to George. Can you find anything out?"

"I'll try. His change of heart is puzzling. Say, if you two are still in the shop when you close up on Tuesday, I should like to come by and join you to walk to the Suffrage event at Memorial Hall. Are we expecting a good crowd?"

"We managed to secure Jane Addams to speak at the meeting!"

"That's quite an accomplishment. I know she spoke at events in Wellington, Winfield, and Girard."

"We're delighted," Kathryn said.

"Well then, I look forward to Tuesday."

They continued to the place where George's friend would pick them up to take them back into town.

CHAPTER EIGHT

June 1912

Feud

"Someone is taking the event posters down," said George as he entered the bookshop the next Tuesday.

"Oh, dear!" said Mary.

"I saw two men assisting Margarete putting one back up on North Main. And they're still up on Memorial Hall's doors."

Mary sighed relief. "Bless those good men."

"Oh yes," Kathryn said, "and Margarete."

A minute later, Mary and Kathryn closed up the shop and they walked a few blocks with George to the ornate Memorial Hall. A line of mostly of women waited to enter. A few men were there, some waiting with them, others gawking at the crowd. Among the gawkers, Markley and Miller stood to one side. They appeared to be arguing, while Miller shouted insults at the people gathered there. Kathryn's group went closer and she could hear some of it.

"Those men are traitors," Miller said to Markley.

"No they're not," Markley said.

"To think that anyone could accept the idea of a woman voting in a federal or state election is ridiculous. Let them be satisfied with voting for school district trustees. Why wasn't this event shut down in the first place?"

"I don't agree with that," Markley said, "but they have a right to free speech."

"The Constitution says all *men* are created equal!" Miller said.

"Now you know it refers to *all* people."

Miller threw his arms up. "*All* people? Even Indians?"

Summer 1866

At the foot of a hill, young Freddie Markley hopped from the wagon as Pa unhitched the horses.

It was hot out here on the prairie and the woods were some distance away, as was the grassy summit up toward top of the hill. Freddie wanted the adventure of climbing up to the rocky rim.

Ma joined Pa. "What're we going to do?" she asked.

"Axle's broke," Pa said, waving his hand at the wagon's wheels. He pointed over toward a line of trees. "There's that creek over there. I'm going to take the horses and water them, then go into that town, Sycamore Falls, and try to sell them. Maybe I can afford to buy a cow and a steer or a bull. Maybe some seed if there's fertile land here."

"Get a milk cow," Ma insisted.

"You'll have to take care of it while I work on building us a house. Meanwhile, we can sleep in the wagon. The cover's still good." He led the horses toward the tree-lined creek. Freddie hopped around on some of the rocky outcrops and ran a ways up the hill where he could look out over the trees that lined the creek to the hills beyond. When Pa emerged from the trees with the horses, Freddie skipped down the hill.

When Freddie reached Ma and the broken wagon, Pa returned with the horses.

"Boy," Pa said to Freddie, "you ride Jack, I'll take Rocky and we'll ride into town."

Freddie and Pa rode to the woods, to the creek where the horses drank again, getting their fill of the clear water. Freddie and Pa rode along the rocky creek. The trees grew thicker along the banks. Freddie gazed up at the towering foliage.

"Keep your eyes ahead, Boy, or a branch'll surely knock you to the ground and I ain't helping you up."

"I'm sorry, Pa, I'll be careful; there's so much to see here."

"Let's go," Pa said as he steered Rocky through a thinning of trees toward open prairie.

As they emerged from the woods, Freddie asked, "Pa, is this our land now?"

"It sure is and we'll make good use of it."

"How did we get the land, Pa?"

"Well, Boy, the government set up this thing called the Homestead Act for people to get free land if they make good use of it. It used to belong to the Indians."

"Do Indians still live around here?"

"A few, but they're mostly gone."

"What happened to them?"

"The government moved them to the Oklahoma territory."

"Why?"

"So we could get this land."

Freddie imagined Native American people riding in a wagon away from here. "Do Indians have boys like me?"

"They sure do. Boys and girls."

"Did the Indian boys and girls move to that other territory in wagons like how we moved here?"

"No, the government made them walk."

"Is it far away?"

"Yes."

Young Freddie imagined a Native American brother and sister both in tears being forced to walk from here with their parents and siblings, the kids sadly looking back as they left their home.

1912

Markley stepped in front of Miller, blocking his view of the crowd.

"I don't know if I should patronize your store anymore," Miller said. "I don't like your attitude."

"Then good riddance. I don't like your attitude, either," Markley said, turning to leave.

* * *

The next day.

It was that time of year. Rain storms could appear without warning. In the mild temperature, the light rain and breeze was somewhat pleasant, and Kathryn gathered her cape against a chill. Cars splashed through puddles up and down Main Street. Some of the cars traveled at speeds she couldn't imagine as safe.

When she walked past Schmidt's Clothing and Shoe, a car splashed her; she tripped and fell. Someone shouted at her from the car as they car sped away.

A man rushed to help her up. "He did that on purpose!" the man shouted. "He veered toward you and aimed for that puddle. Are you all right?"

Kathryn thanked him as she tried to brush herself off. He offered a clean handkerchief which she accepted to wipe off her face.

"Do you own the Main Street Bookshop?"

"I co-own it with Mary Dodd."

"I am headed there to meet with Miss Dodd about stereographic photograph cards. I am Mr. Carter. I'll walk with you."

"Oh, do you sell them?"

"I create and sell them. I'm a photographer from Wichita and I set up around the Flint Hills."

Kathryn and Mary had considered selling that type of card of area hills, that perhaps there was a market for that. They offered some postcards at the shop, but this kind of card was so popular these days. They could enhance their offerings.

CHAPTER NINE

June 1912

A Sermon and Women's Club

On Sunday, Mary and Kathryn stepped out the church's double doors and remained in line to greet the Reverend Bruce. A young woman was in line just ahead, talking with him.

"I certainly enjoyed your sermon today," she said. "I know there are differing opinions these days."

Reverend Bruce smiled. "Femininity is natural and good for women as it plays an important part in the roles of the sexes."

She nodded.

John Shane, who was in line behind her said, "I agree with the young lady, Reverend."

Kathryn looked for Anna, but she wasn't with John. Mary turned to Kathryn.

"Anna and Mr. Shane must not be public yet," she whispered.

"I haven't seen them out," said Kathryn.

As the line continued to move, an acquaintance of Kathryn's, named Rose, walked up to Kathryn and looked for a place in line. Kathryn smiled and let her in between Mary and her.

They reached a small group of men that had just gathered. Fred Markley, John Shane, and Theodore Miller excused themselves and stepped aside, so the women could pass.

"Good morning, Rose," Reverend Bruce said when she, Mary, and Kathryn reached him. "Haven't seen you lately. Everything all right?"

Rose smiled. "Oh yes. I was under the weather a little, but doing well now, thank you."

Reverend Bruce winked and smiled. "Glad to hear it."

"I appreciated your sermon today," she said.

Kathryn avoided the gender role topic when she reached Reverend Bruce, as did Mary.

Kathryn had no doubts about his views on Suffrage. Some clergy approved of it, but not Reverend Bruce.

When the line broke up, Mary and Kathryn stepped out onto the front lawn. The ample spring rains had greened everything up well.

"It's so nice out," said Mary, "let's take a walk around town."

Kathryn agreed and they went out to the sidewalk. The warm spring smells were everywhere as they started along Fifth Street. After about a block, Rose caught up to them.

"Good afternoon," she said.

They returned the greeting. Kathryn introduced them and Rose watched all around as she walked alongside them.

"Are you looking for someone?" Kathryn asked.

"No, but I wanted to ask you, Kathryn, if I may pay you a visit to discuss something that I know you're involved with."

"I would love to have you over," Kathryn said. "Perhaps this afternoon?"

"I'm afraid I can't this afternoon, but maybe tomorrow around noon for a short time if I'm not imposing?"

"Tomorrow at noon is fine." Kathryn looked at Mary.

"Of course, Kathryn. I'll keep shop then."

Kathryn looked forward to getting to know Rose better.

Rose expressed thanks and left in the opposite direction.

A car skidded to a stop and they turned to see a man helping Rose up off the street. She appeared unhurt, but Mary and Kathryn rushed to her and helped her up.

Rose caught her breath. "I'm fine. I tripped."

"You shouldn't run out into the street like that," the man said. "Thank God you're all right."

Rose nodded. "I'm sorry. I should be more careful."

"Where were you going in such a hurry, running like that?" he said.

"Nowhere special. I just need to get home right away," she said.

"Perhaps I can take you there," the man said.

"No thank you. I live only three blocks from here." Rose continued to pant, skipped across the street to the sidewalk, and went home.

Mary and Kathryn went on, both of them relieved but upset by the incident.

"Maybe Rose'll tell you tomorrow what that was all about," said Mary. "Why she's in a hurry to get home.'

* * *

The next day, Kathryn invited Rose in.

"My husband doesn't know I'm here," Rose said.

They settled in the living room.

"I didn't know you are married," Kathryn said.

Rose smiled, a bit embarrassed. "Yes, I am Mrs. John Shane."

Kathryn suppressed a gasp but managed a smile. "Well, Mrs. Shane, what can I do for you?"

"I heard Ida is forming a Women's Club soon and it may deal with Suffrage. I don't have many opportunities to socialize with other women or participate in Suffrage activities."

"I'm sorry to have eavesdropped," Kathryn said, "but I heard your comment yesterday to the Reverend Bruce that you appreciated his sermon opposing Suffrage."

"I have to keep my feelings to myself. John was nearby and he's adamantly opposed to Suffrage."

"Is he?" Kathryn almost let it slip that John and Anna attended their event planning meeting together. "I see. I'm sure you can join and we can find a way to keep it discreet."

"I would appreciate that."

"If I'm not prying, what were you in such a hurry about yesterday?"

"It was nothing. I didn't want John to wonder why I wasn't home preparing Sunday dinner."

Kathryn nodded. "I will ask Ida to invite you to join the Women's Club."

"Wonderful, but not through mail correspondence, please."

"Of course not."

* * *

John Shane dropped Rose off in front of Ida's house. She climbed the porch steps to where Kathryn, Mary and others were sitting.

"Mr. Shane is in full support of me joining the Women's Club," she said as John drove away. "No secrecy necessary. We had a discussion and I explained that these clubs have existed for a long time inolving such issues as education, child labor, and library creation. 'Quite worthwhile,' he told me. In fact, he thinks it'll occupy me enough to stay out of the Suffrage Movement."

Everyone laughed. "Quite correct," Ida said. "You told him the truth."

"The lilacs are still blooming," she said. She invited everyone to follow her down the porch steps. "Come with me."

They all went down around the porch to the south side of the house and gathered next to the waist-high violet-colored blooms.

"I love this," Kathryn said, taking in the sweet scent. The others leaned into the shrubs and echoed her.

Ida stepped out to the sunny lawn and took in the warm spring sunshine.

Mary and Kathryn joined her.

"You really are fixated on that hill," Mary said to Kathryn.

"The view from there must be magnificent. If I get a chance, I know I can climb to the top."

Ida put her hand on Kathryn's shoulder and changed the subject as the others gathered around. "With the Equal Suffrage Amendment to the Kansas Constitution on the ballot this coming November, we have a lot going for us. Governor Stubbs's support for Suffrage and the Men's League for Woman Suffrage that was organized in April gained thousands of Kansas men in sympathy with the Movement. Some men are helping talk to people we women can't approach. You're all aware of the barber shop incident with George Fielding?"

"Terrible," Mary said.

"We have a lot of work to do by November," said Ida. "There's a parade next month and I have a project inside for us."

Yards of material sat on Ida's dining room table with needles and thread. She and Margarete arranged chairs around to allow room to work.

Kathryn started on a banner and sewed some pre-cut letters to spell "Women Vote."

After a while, Ida stood. "I'm afraid we're depleting the treasury," she said. "We're getting something from the Kansas Equal Suffrage Association, but we have to spend wisely. The Association can't manage all 105 counties and we have to do some fundraising.

"What can we do?" asked Mary.

"Balloon sales are doing well in some towns, including Mound Grove," said Kathryn.

"What kind of balloons?" asked Rose.

"Large ones, two feet wide lettered with 'Votes for Women' and 'Votes for Mother.' They're selling them on the street and designating 'Balloon Day'."

"We can start helping by having a successful parade and have our vendors on the sidewalk," said Ida.

A car pulled up out front. Rose went to look out the front window.

"I have to go, everyone. I'm sorry, I don't want John to come in and see what we're doing."

"Of course, Rose," said Ida.

The others hurried Rose to the front door and she stepped onto the porch. John got out of the car and leaned against it.

"Bye, everyone! Thank you!" Rose called in through the open front door.

She went down the steps to John.

CHAPTER TEN

July 1912

Main Street, Sycamore Falls

Kathryn's group rode in an open car along Main Street displaying bright yellow "Women Vote" banners and balloons as the car puttered along with George driving. She didn't recognize many spectators lining the parade route. A few carried large balloons or signs that said, "Votes for Mother," but not everyone showed support.

"Not in Sycamore Falls!" yelled some men.

Some women shouted as well. "Embrace your femininity!"

More men shouted.

"Politics are improper for women!"

"Voting might cause you to grow a beard!"

They rolled by the largest crowd on the lawn of the courthouse square.

Marching women from Wichita and other cities around Kansas joined local women.

Mary took a tomato to the cheek. Charles Dodd rushed toward the offender.

Theodore Miller stood with the crowd lining the street and shouted, "You're not switching over and supporting them now, are you, Dodd?"

"I'm going to defend my daughter, Miller! Look what they're doing!"

Dodd stepped into the street and yelled at the hecklers.

Markley stood among a group of men in front of the National Association Opposed to Woman Suffrage office, a couple of the younger men pointing at their NAOWS banner.

CHAPTER ELEVEN

Late November 1912

Kansas Suffrage

K ansas voters passed Suffrage on November 5, 1912.

About three weeks later, Kathryn, Mary, and George found themselves walking along West Hill Road.

"I brought champagne glasses and a small bottle of grape juice," said Mary.

Kathryn felt hesitant to go as George led them through the break in the fence onto Markley's property. She kept picturing Markley, gun loaded, crouching behind a tree, but as they hiked along the trail, they had the woods to themselves.

The crunch of leaves behind them made Kathryn jump.

"Deer," said Mary.

"I'm sorry," Kathryn said, "I'm on edge."

"As long as we don't stray from where he's authorized, we're fine," said George.

Kathryn limped along the trail with them to where it opened onto tallgrass prairie and they helped her up a short grassy rise. Up here, she saw a clearing in a mostly wooded area.

George pointed toward it. "Let's head down there."

Sugar Loaf stood tall to the left and the summit beckoned.

Kathryn stopped and gazed up. "I can almost touch the hilltop," she said. "It must be beautiful up there."

"Let's go on," George said, starting down to the clearing. Mary took Kathryn's arm and helped her along the way.

They reached clutter surrounded by overgrown grass and partially buried by sediment.

"An old covered wagon," Kathryn said.

"I think they had to abandon it," George said.

"And some of the contents," said Mary.

"Wooden barrel staves without the metal hoops," Kathryn said. "Part of a plow and I think that was a butter churn. What do you suppose that big metal box was?"

"A stove," Mary said.

"They had to leave some of their possessions," said George, "but I assume the plow was useless if they decided to settle here what with all the rocks." He pointed toward a tree-lined creek. "Unless there's good ground over there. He turned toward the little trail. "Let's take our picnic up to that level area before the rocks. It's not far, Kathryn."

"Is that something we should do?" asked Mary.

"I can make it," Kathryn said. "I've found a way of swinging my leg out that works."

When they reached the level area, the sound of a shotgun "pow" sent them diving to the ground. George poked his head up. "Markley! He's up on the Promontory."

A lone figure stood beneath the grove of trees, then he yelled. "That's far enough, Fielding! You and your female cohorts can stay on that spot now, but the rest of this hill is off limits!"

Kathryn was glad for the brief rest. She made the best of this and gazed out at the view, even if they were only partway up Sugar Loaf.

George waved at Markley. They started back downhill.

"I wonder if we could stick to the original plan to have our picnic near the old wagon," Kathryn said.

"We need to head on," said George. "He's asserting his authority and ownership."

"I know I could have made it to that Promontory," Kathryn said.

As they walked, Mary said, "I wonder what happened."

"I think I know," said George.

"We haven't reached the top, but at least we made it onto the hill," said Mary.

"I'm so glad we did," said Kathryn. "Now that I've had a try at this, I'm ready to plan a trip to Washington, DC, for the big Suffrage parade in March. Please come over to my house to plan after Christmas."

CHAPTER TWELVE

February 27, 1913

On a Train in Illinois

"I have never seen tree limbs down like this," Kathryn said, looking at broken down trees throughout the woodlands in central Illinois.

"I read about it," said Margarete. "They had a terrible ice storm last Friday." She pointed out the window at the telephone poles along the track. "Some of the wires are down."

They passed a pole with a lineman near its top working on a connection.

"I have an idea," Mary said as she reached into the guitar case under her seat, pulling out some sheet music, and turned to Kathryn.

"Please hold this sheet for me," she said, retrieving her guitar from its case.

"Oh! Are you going to sing for us?" Kathryn asked excitedly as she looked around at the other passengers.

"It's called, 'Eliza Jane'. This was published last year and I bought the music as soon as it was available."

"I know the song," said Margarete.

"Sing with me," said Mary.

Margarete and Kathryn traded seats and Margarete sat with Mary and guitar, holding the sheet music for her, and together they sang—

Eliza Jane she had a wheel, its rim was painted red;
Eliza had another wheel that turned inside her head.
She put the two together, she gave them both a whirl,
And now she rides the Parkway sides a Twentieth Century Girl.

"Oh, have you seen Eliza Jane a-cycling in the park?
"Oh, have you seen Eliza Jane?" The people all remark.
They shout 'Hi! hi!' as she rides by; the little doggies bark,
For we all have a pain when Eliza Jane goes cycling in the park.

No more do skirts unfold her, tho' much her papa grieves,
But baggy trousers hold her in their big pneumatic sleeves;
For where you see the bloomers bloom she sits her wheel astride. . .

*   * * ***

This is her emancipation year, the woman movement's on. . .

They cheered lightly as the song ended, which caused a commotion within their car. A few women and men cast disapproving looks, but two women from several seats ahead shuffled their way back to Kathryn and friends.

"That was lovely," said one who called herself Judith.

"Fabulous," said her traveling companion, Pearl. "To where are you traveling?"

"Washington, D.C.," Kathryn said.

Judith and Pearl lit up with excitement. "To the Suffrage parade!" they said in unison.

All laughed and Mary said, "The very thing!"

"Where are you from?" Kathryn asked.

"Denver," said Pearl. "And you?"

"Sycamore Falls, Kansas."

"Say, congratulations on passing Suffrage in Kansas last November!" said Judith.

"You beat us to the punch by eleven years," said Kathryn.

"I had thought Kansas would beat us," said Pearl.

"It's been a long, hard fight," said Kathryn.

A man across the aisle stepped over. "And the fight will continue," he said.

"Well," Kathryn started, but she realized he was in support of the Movement by his expression.

George shuffled back to them and said to the man, "Any support will be essential, don't you agree, sir?"

The man nodded and extended his hand to George. "It certainly is. And I am Gregory Wade."

"George Fielding."

The conductor entered the car and came over to them.

"Ladies and sirs, I received complaints about the ladies' disorderly conduct. It's only fair to inform you that as we pass through Illinois, a conductor is vested by state law with police powers. You must not continue this behavior or I will expel you from the train at the next stop."

Some of the same disapproving passengers smiled and looked away from them as the conductor turned to exit the car.

"We weren't disorderly," mumbled Kathryn. "Some sap didn't like our opinions and falsely reported us."

"To be so dishonest," Mary said.

"Isn't that the whole struggle?" Kathryn said. "According to one politician, this I read: 'Politics is no place for women. The men are able to run the government and take care of the women.'"

"Yeah, the whole struggle," agreed Judith and Pearl.

"Oh yeah," said the rest of them, along with George and Gregory.

The rest of the ride to Indianapolis was uneventful and they all spent the night at boarding houses near the depot.

* * *

The next morning, as they rolled into eastern Indiana, they took over the back of the train car with their new friends, Pearl, Judith, Gregory and his wife, Harriet. George sat in the seat across the aisle from Mary and Kathryn. He had established a rapport with Gregory and Harriet in a nearby seat.

Kathryn leaned over to Mary. "Were you up late last night?"

"I certainly was. George and I sat up talking late into the night before he headed over to the men's boarding house."

"Scandalous," Kathryn said.

Mary giggled and smiled over at George.

They continued through Indiana and a while after crossing into Ohio, they held onto their seats as the train started to slow and the conductor stepped into the car.

"Next stop, Dayton," he said. "Next stop, Dayton. No disembarking unless this is your stop."

They came to a full stop next to the depot and a small crowd of women and men stood on the platform waiting to board.

The door wooshed open. The conductor ushered the group into the forward section amid chatter and chuckling.

Margarete glanced at the group. "We have competition"

"Allies," Kathryn said. "I shall go introduce myself."

"That's just like you," said Margarete.

Kathryn went up to sit with the group. It wasn't long before she and one of the women were hobbling back.

They took a seat in front of Margarete and Mary.

"Margarete, Mary," said Kathryn, "I'd like to introduce Katharine Wright from Dayton. She's very involved in the Dayton Suffrage Movement."

Everyone exchanged greetings and George joined them.

"It appears," said Katharine Wright, "that we are going to the same event."

"I think there'll be a good turnout," said Kathryn.

"We're hopeful. And isn't there an upcoming Dayton march?" said Kathryn.

"We're organizing that for next year in the fall."

"Wonderful," said Kathryn. "Are you getting support for it?"

"Hundreds so far are interested in marching, even my brother Orville will join us, as will our father."

"I wish I could join you then," Kathryn said, "but I'm afraid one long trip every couple of years is my limit with my leg as it is."

George came over and introduced himself.

"I teach high school Civics in Kansas," he said.

"And I teach high school Latin and English in Dayton," Katharine Wright said, smiling.

"Well then," he said to her, "perhaps we'll see you at the march."

"I hope so," Katharine Wright said as she excused herself and returned to her friends at the front of the car.

"Well," Kathryn said, "she's from a famous family."

"Her brother," Margarete said, "isn't the only famous person who'll be marching in the parade."

"I expect there will be other famous people in the Washington parade," said Mary.

"There will," said Kathryn. "Someone I've long wanted to meet."

CHAPTER THIRTEEN

March 3, 1913

The Great Women's Suffrage Parade
Washington, DC

Kathryn hobbled along with her friends and thousands of marchers on Pennsylvania Avenue, some women on horseback leading, others walking with signs.

"Word is to maintain a dignified manner as we march," Kathryn said.

Margarete was a few paces ahead, and she pointed to a woman wearing a crown and a long white cape riding a large white horse.

"Do you know who that is!" Margarete shouted back. "That's Inez Milholland Boissevain leading the parade!" She then pointed ahead beyond Milholland. "How are we going to get this parade started with those swarms of people crowding the street ahead!"

Women toward the front shouted at the hoards to clear the way. Kathryn and her companions joined in.

"Clear the way!" Kathryn shouted, lobbing a rolled up poster ahead.

One man turned back toward them and shouted: "We're honoring our new president!"

"We've had the street reserved!" Kathryn shouted.

"Show some respect for Mr. Wilson's inaugural or go away!"

A couple of women ahead of them continued the shouting.

They started moving; marchers at the front bunched up until the hoard parted enough for them to proceed single file.

Margarete reached the gap lined by men. Ten steps in, a spectator tripped her and she tumbled flat on her face. Mary and other marchers rushed to help her up. After she regained her balance, they pushed forward. A man reached in and groped Mary. She swatted him away and he laughed. "Go away, you pug-ugly girl."

"Leave her alone!" shouted Margarete.

"Shut up, dumb Dora!" another man shouted as he attempted to grope her.

Others lining the way laughed. Kathryn spotted two policemen. "Please, sirs!" she shouted over the jeering.

The cops laughed along with other jeering men. One cop yelled, "Go home where you belong!"

A man jumped in front of Kathryn. "How about a little kiss and I'll let you pass."

Kathryn shouldered him to the side and he stumbled.

He grabbed her arm and pushed her onto the street. "Don't shove me, woman! Who're you going to trip with that leg?"

An officer stepped in and pulled the man aside, then helped Kathryn to her feet. "You made it more difficult. It'd have been easier for you if you'd relented," he said.

"No!" Kathryn shouted.

"Go on, then." He left and returned to the side crowd.

George was several rows back and pushed his way forward.

One man shouted: "You sap! Where's your skirt!" Followed by several of them shouting, "Henpecko!" Other male marchers behind George got the same treatment.

More laughter and jeering from the sidelines.

An African-American woman marched with the Mississippi group. A couple of marchers near them shouted to her to go to the back in the "Negro women's section." People on the sidelines yelled at her as well. "Go to the back where you belong!"

Mary rushed over to her and got in front of the jeering marchers.

"What's wrong with you! Our non-white sisters deserve the right to vote! Her struggle has been worse than ours!"

The marchers tried to ignore Mary. Kathryn wanted to join her, but the crowd was too thick for her to move sideways with her leg so she cupped her hands and yelled over as loudly as she could manage: "We succeed when we join all women and men together!"

Margarete grabbed Kathryn's hand and they both raised their arms to show support. One white woman went to the African-American woman and took her hand to march together. Kathryn yelled: "She deserves racial equality!"

Mary returned through the chaos and took Kathryn's arm and they forged ahead.

"There's Helen Keller!" Mary shouted, pointing to a woman toward the front of the line. Assaulting hands groped Helen and she stumbled. Other marchers helped her up as spectators continued accosting her.

A minute later, Margarete said, "Oh dear! She's on the verge of collapse, panting up a storm!"

"Oh, poor Helen!" Kathryn said. "Look at those scratches on her face and elbows. I think she skinned her knee when that sap tripped her!"

Mary pulled Kathryn along to catch up to Helen, who accepted Kathryn's arm.

Helen and Kathryn labored their way forward as they continued to press on.

A police officer crossed in front. Kathryn waved, getting his attention, and he came toward her. "Sir, please, look what they've done!"

He regarded Helen, then turned to Kathryn. "Nothing like this would be happening if you would stay at home!"

"So I've heard!" shouted Kathryn.

Kathryn and companions emerged from the passage inadvertently blocking Woodrow Wilson's entourage. They could see President-elect Wilson and the presidential party a few blocks ahead where the street was more clear, arriving to little celebration of any kind. A look of surprise and disappointment showed on Wilson's face and those with him.

CHAPTER FOURTEEN

April 1913

Late Evening, Ida's Porch

Margarete arrived at Ida's in a flurry of excitement and joined the others on the south porch, showing them a March 8th copy of *Woman's World and Suffrage News*.

"We made the front page!" she said.

Kathryn held it close. Under the headline, "Parade Struggles to Victory Despite Disgraceful Scenes" were several parade photos.

"Look, Kathryn," Margarete said. "The inset photo—there's Mary and that's your sleeve."

Kathryn laughed. "No mistaking it, that's my sleeve."

"But Mary's there!" Margarete said.

Mary leaned over. "Oh yes! There! And there's Kathryn's foot at an angle."

"Now, that I recognize," Kathryn said.

* * *

They stayed until after sundown. As twilight faded, everyone followed Kathryn to the railing. She leaned out and gazed out at the full Moon high above the land, shedding its ghostly brilliance over the hills. Rose went and stood next to her.

"I'm glad you made it," said Kathryn.

"John has an appointment this evening, I think he's meeting Mr. Markley at the Prairie Room Club."

"It almost looks like daytime out there under a bright Moon like this, doesn't it?" said Kathryn.

"That's very like you to say something like that," said Mary.

"Well, it gets me thinking," said Kathryn.

"What about?" asked Rose.

"Have you read *From the Earth to the Moon* by Jules Verne?"

"I have," said Ida. "Quite an impossible trip."

"Is it really?" said Kathryn.

"Human beings can never leave Earth to travel up such a distance."

"Didn't people say that about flying? And we have airplanes now."

"Getting to the Moon is a different matter."

"What about Suffrage?" Kathryn countered. "Did many think Kansas would pass it? When people put their minds to a goal, they get results."

"Men mostly achieve inventions."

"Not all are by men," insisted Kathryn. "There are some inventions by women. In fact, a woman invented the locomotive chimney stack thirty or forty years ago. And the ice cream maker was invented by Nancy Johnson years ago, around mid-last century. And besides, some men inventors have supported Suffrage. Orville Wright marched alongside his sister Katharine in Washington, remember?" She stared up at the slowly arcing Moon. "When there's a common goal and enough people work toward it, it can be realized. Like votes for women."

"There's a better chance in that than reaching the Moon," said Ida.

"Sometimes I wonder," said Rose.

The others echoed "yes we will" while Kathryn gazed out. There was Sugar Loaf basking in the moonlight beckoning her even now.

The sound of wheels on gravel interrupted her thoughts and car lanterns appeared on the gravel drive up from west Hill Road.

"Could that be our new member?" said Mary.

"She won't make it tonight," said Ida. "I think that's Lewis coming back to take you all home when it's time. Until then, I don't think we have much more business so enjoy the Moon and the nice evening weather."

Meanwhile

"Oooo, I have a chill," she said as she sat with him on Sugar Loaf's Promontory.

He opened his jacket and wrapped it and his arm around her shoulders, pulling her close.

She snuggled into his warmth and sighed. "So lovely in the moonlight," she said. She then pointed to a hilltop house glowing in the moonlight. "Look over there."

"That's Lewis and Ida's place," he said.

"I was supposed to be there."

"Maybe it's good you're not. *She* is there. I mean... never mind."

"Who?"

"—Uh, my sister. She's not in with the Suffrage stuff but she's seeing what it's all about. I expect she'll have disagreements with the ladies in attendance there."

She slid a hand around his chest. "I'd rather be up here with you."

CHAPTER FIFTEEN

July 1914

Elm River South of Sycamore Falls

On a hot 1914 summer day along the calm waters of the river, Alan rowed the canoe toward the river bank where they stopped under an overhang of foliage. John Shane held on as Alan abruptly steered the boat out from under the tree.

"Snake up there," Alan said, "don't want it dropping on us."

They went to the middle of the river and John sat back. "Say, there's a lot going on in Europe," he said.

Alan nodded. "Yeah, I read that Austria-Hungary declared war on Serbia, maybe in response to the assassination of Franz and Sophie Ferdinand last month, but probably not that simple."

"As long as we don't get involved, let them fight it out."

"War's never good. People will die," said Alan.

"We need to stay out of it," John said.

"Right. Let's get our fishing gear out."

Alan rowed a little more. John steadied himself and cast his line out.

"That's a fine bait casting rod," said Alan.

"Rose gave it to me for my birthday."

"She seems like a nice woman, although I don't see her out much. Violette says she only sees her occasionally out for groceries and she's not in any ladies' organizations that Violette's noticed."

"She stays home mostly."

"Don't you let her go out?"

"No—I mean, where'd you hear that? That's not true."

"I was kidding."

"But I have to level with you, Alan. I'm really bored with her and I'm even a little embarrassed to be out with her."

"Even to dinner or to the park?"

"Hm, yeah, the park."

"The park's nice! Take her on a picnic there."

"And do what?"

"I'm sorry, I know it's none of my business. I hope you're all fine."

"She doesn't help things with her constant mumbling about Woman Suffrage."

"Violette talks about it, too. I don't much like it, either, but don't worry about it. It'll fade away once women get the picture that it'll never pass at the Federal level."

"I'm less optimistic than you."

"Would it be so bad if it did?"

"I doubt you when you say things like that, Alan. A real man stands up to things like this."

"All right. Back to your problem. You have that fancy car and you've got money. Why not take Rose out some place special in Wichita?"

"I'm just never in the mood to go. I work hard selling investments to make saps like you rich."

"Heh-heh. I'll give you that, except when you based my portfolio on the Dow Jones back in oh-seven. I lost a lot that year."

"Everybody did. It bounced back. You listened to me and didn't sell as I advised and you kept your shirt."

"Anyway, just friendly advice. Violette and I do a lot together and it keeps us going and I'm not eyeing the pretty girls at church like I see you doing."

"Drop the subject."

"All right. Let's find where the fish are biting." Alan rowed the canoe to a fallen tree sitting across the water near the bank.

CHAPTER SIXTEEN

September 1914

Opposition

At the Prairie Room Club, John Shane leaned forward in his chair. "Did you hear that the French and British defeated the German army along the Marne River in France?"

Markley and Miller both sat up.

"I heard about it," Miller said.

"As I've said," Shane said, "let them fight it out over there."

"Right. You've said that," Markley said.

"Let's hope they fight out the whole mess quickly," Shane said.

Markley offered a light to Miller's cigar. "Let's end *our* little war and be friends again, Theodore."

Miller puffed the cigar. "That's all I want, Fred."

"I mean, we've got a common enemy, a common goal."

"Hear, hear," said John Shane.

"Well, John," said Miller, "what about that girlfriend of yours? You think Rose doesn't know?"

"I prefer 'mistress' to 'girlfriend'. If she knows about her, she isn't letting on. Besides, if Rose divorces me, where's she going to go? Alimony won't enable her to live the life she has now. In case you gentlemen haven't noticed, I'm raking it in. I might even be as rich as you in a few years."

"I've seen you driving that new Packard," Markley said. "For what you paid, you could have had a Dodge for each day of the week and money left over. Those Dodges are nice cars. I'll grant you a Dodge isn't a Packard, but at least it beats a Model T hands down. Anyway, I think your wife *could* find a decent husband."

"She'd have a better chance than that bookshop keeper," Miller said. "The one with the bum leg."

"Nobody will want that woman," Shane said.

"You know," Markley said, "if she'd quit that Suffragette nonsense, she wouldn't be half bad."

"If she wasn't so anti-lady," Miller said, "she wouldn't be in the predicament she's in. At home instead of climbing on rocks above my place would have been safer for her."

Shane mumbled, "Uh huh."

"She managed that march in Washington all right," said Markley. "The little gal's probably getting stronger I guess. She wants to try climbing up my hill again, I'm sure."

"I can't understand why someone like her chooses a hard life when she shouldn't have to," Miller said. "By the way, Fred, there's that photographer, Carter from Wichita who's here photographing around the area. Is he going up on your hill?"

"At some point. What about the craggy hill above your place?"

"That's public land so I don't know. He can go up there if he wants."

"It should be called Wolfe Hill," Shane said, chuckling.

"So are you going to allow her onto more of your land, Fred?" Miller asked.

"I am considering it."

"Don't encourage her."

"I have some respect for her as a businesswoman. Maybe I'll give her a little freedom up there and let her fail. Could be she'll give up and realize her quest is futile."

"Like Suffrage," Miller said, "Did you hear Nevada and Montana might adopt it?"

"I read about it; I hope not," Shane said. "If they do, a few western states won't steer the nation."

"Like Kansas," Miller said.

"We didn't try hard enough and lost Kansas," Markley said, "but we need to stay active with the NAOWS and recruit more men. We're up against that National Federation of Women's Clubs."

"Men are still the primary voters and we need more of them in the NAOWS," Shane said.

"What about that school teacher?" Miller said. "I'll make you a deal, Fred. You invite him to join the Prairie Club and if he does, we'll work on him to join us in the NAOWS."

"Is he a Prairie Room Club sort of man?" Shane asked.

"He might be," Markley said. "I know him pretty well and his principal, Vern Holt, is a member here. Holt came to an NAOWS meeting a couple of weeks ago."

"But you've denied Fielding access to most of your land now and he's probably not happy with you."

"I could bribe him to join by offering hill access again if you bring him here."

"What about the bookshop keeper?"

"Additional bribing to get George Fielding to join by offering her access."

"I've got better ways to increase membership to NAOWS," Miller said.

"Such as?" Shane said. "Suffrage has made its gains, but I don't expect to see it pass nationwide in my lifetime."

"I've got a plan," Miller said, looking as if he had something to hide.

"Don't do anything rash," Markley said.

CHAPTER SEVENTEEN

October 1914

Invite

When Kathryn got back to the bookshop after lunch, George came in and went around to the new books display table. He tapped his fingers on a copy of *A Short History of Women's Rights, From the Days of Augustus to the Present Time.* "Two more states might pass Suffrage," he said. "Montana and Nevada."

"That would be fantastic for our future," said Kathryn.

"Indeed," said George, "and I have my own possible future development. Deciding if it's a good thing or not."

"Do tell," said Kathryn.

Someone came into the bookshop.

"Hello Violette," said George.

She smiled. "You're leaning on just the book I came here for," she said.

Kathryn was about to go greet her, but George took one of the books and handed it to her.

She flipped through it. "This will do nicely. It's not at the library yet and with Mr. Stephens on an outing this weekend, I'll finally have a chance to read it."

"George," said Mary quietly from behind the counter, "what is your 'development'?"

"It's all right if Violette knows," he said to Mary. "It seems Mr. Markley wants to make amends."

"Make amends?" said Violette.

"I used to go trailing on his property and he suddenly forbade me from there recently. Now he has invited me to join the Prairie Room Club."

"Will you?" asked Violette. "Mr. Holt is a member."

"I'm aware of that. That could be a bit awkward. He and I don't always see eye to eye on things."

"But I know he likes you," she said.

"That's not obvious to me. I'm not sure yet about joining. It's not a place I've aspired to getting involved with. It's a fine club and I guess I'll consider it."

* * *

When George entered the dark paneled room, he glanced around at the mounted deer and other trophy kills. A fire roared in the fireplace and he sank into the soft chair across from Fred Markley, denying the offer of a cigar and a beer. Mr. Markley apparently wasn't aware that teachers were discouraged from smoking or drinking.

"I appreciate the invitation to join you here this evening," said George.

"Glad to have you, George. I don't have anything planned for our little meeting, just relax and chat for a bit. You know, I was a bit hasty in denying you access to my hill. I think we can go back to the way we were. What do you think? It's a good thing that someone appreciates that hill like you do. There's some history there, you know."

"There certainly is."

"Now, there's something I've wanted to ask you. It's no secret I'm not in full support of Women's Suffrage. Mrs. Markley is a little, but then, many women are, not surprisingly—although some oppose it and I can understand their reasoning. Why, they're afraid it's an assault on womanhood, cherished men's and women's roles in society. Experts think the divorce rate will jump dramatically. Did you know the NAOWS was started by a woman? Women are already equal to men, just in different spheres and women don't need to be able to vote. Take those two women bookshop owners. They stayed in business even during hard economic times a couple of years ago. Most impressive. They didn't need to vote to attain that success. Indeed, many a voting man went bankrupt then."

George nodded without actually agreeing. After a few more minutes, he pulled out his watch and prepared to leave.

"Thank you for meeting me here," Markley said. "I'll get back to you later about access to the hill. It might be a while."

George thanked him and left.

Markley also left the Prairie Room Club and decided to go for a walk. He headed down Main Street. About a block down, he stopped and gazed at the storefront across the street that was once a general store. He remembered an incident near there from when he was a boy every time he saw it, stirring an emotion within him. He missed his mother and wished she'd been better treated by some and appreciated for all she did to raise him and his siblings.

1871

On a June day, fourteen-year-old Fred Markley stood next to his mother in Main Street General Store as she gathered a bundle of fabric that was placed on the counter by the shopkeeper. She handed Fred a bag of flour sitting there.

"Fred," she said, "take this to the wagon and wait for me there. Keep a tight hold on the bag in that wind and try to secure everything in the wagon down. I may want you to ride in the bed of the wagon to keep things from blowing away."

Fred complied and the shop door flew open in the wind as he exited, stepped onto the boardwalk, and leaned into the wind that gusted down Main Street, sending up swirls of dust. Fred held onto the bag and maintained his balance as he made his way to the wagon. A gust almost blew him over, bringing laughter from several men who stood back against a saloon window. Fred reached the wagon and set the bag in it, then went to the horse, steadied him, and gave him a small sugar cube from the shopkeeper.

Commotion across the street diverted his attention.

As Ma emerged cradling a bundle of fabric in her arms against the wind and gathered her shawl closely around her, several of the loitering men started shouting.

"You'll need more than that to cover up!" shouted one.

"The more you cover, the better!" shouted another. "Nothing's going to make you any prettier!"

"You should be home sewing and doing useful things, woman, not out having a good time!" yelled another.

Ma stumbled off the boardwalk as dust blasted into her face.

Fred left the wagon, ran toward her, took her arm, and helped steady her, but another gust pulled her armload of fabric away and sent it flying to the feet of the jeering men. Fred ran toward them. One picked up the bundle and tossed it to one of his companions. Fred lunged for it and one of the men grabbed and held onto it.

"Figured you all wouldn't want this to blow away so we'll keep it safe for you," he said. They all laughed, and the man's hat blew off. Fred lunged for it, snatched it from the air and the man protested.

"Give me back our fabric!" Fred shouted.

The man holding it said, "I think my wife can use this."

"You ain't got no wife," said another.

The man laughed. "If I did, she'd want this."

"Give it back!" yelled Fred.

More laughter as the men tossed the fabric back and forth. One of them held it tightly as Fred tried to pry it from him.

"Give me my hat, boy," he demanded.

Fred threw the man's hat out into the raging wind. The man dropped the bundle and jumped out after the hat tumbling down the dusty street. Fred scooped the fabric bundle up and ran to his mother to help her across as the men tripped over themselves scrambling after the hat.

"Let's go before they get over there," she said.

Fred tried to calm the horse again and they drove down Main Street with the wind at their back.

CHAPTER EIGHTEEN

November 1914

Anti-Suffrage

Kathryn finished shelving some books and opened a letter from Katharine Wright.

Dear Kathryn,
We had our parade in Dayton on October 24th. Over a thousand women and three dozen men marched, including my brother Orville who marched by my side. I am so proud of him. Thousands of spectators on the sidewalks were respectful to us which I found encouraging. Unfortunately, Amendment Three to the Ohio Constitution failed, so Suffrage didn't pass. Our campaign continues.
Be well and carry on.

Cordially yours,
Katharine Wright

She smiled and folded the letter.
As she put it away, Mary burst in the front door. "Kathryn! There's a protest outside!"
Kathryn rushed to her, and Mary led her outside.
"Listen," said Mary.

Shouts came from a few blocks away with one male voice drowning out the rest.

"Somebody's on a megaphone horn," said Mary.

They went toward it and saw Theodore Miller with the horn to his mouth on the courthouse lawn as he was surrounded by two dozen men holding signs that said "THE SUFFRAGETTES ARE DISRUPTING OUR TOWN! JOIN NAOWS!" Crowds of people went by, some stopping.

Miller stepped forward and shouted through the megaphone: "They protest! Now we do! Don't let them! They'll induct your wives and daughters! Their protests will be answered accordingly! Save our women with harsh treatment of Suffragettes! Show them the evil of their ways!"

The protesting men erupted in cheers.

"Women! Do you want to risk what this will do to your marriage? Suffrage is causing strife and more divorces! Don't let it happen to you! All women must oppose Woman Suffrage!

"Fellow citizens! Who do you need to silence? Start with those bookshop keepers! And the Schmidts! Other store owners who support Suffrage! Shut them down and run them out of town! You know who they are!"

* * *

Kathryn got busy herself. A week later, she organized a group of twenty pro-Suffrage women, including Ida and a few men and gathered them on the sidewalk across the street from the NAOWS office early afternoon. They held signs that said: "HOW LONG BEFORE 20,000,000 AMERICAN CITIZENS PARTICIPATE IN DEMOCRACY?"

As cars drove by, the pro-Suffrage demonstrators shouted, "Votes for Women!" Although some motorists showed support, a tomato hit Ida's cheek and bounced over to Kathryn's waist dress.

She took a handkerchief and wiped the bit of tomato off Ida's cheek. "Are you all right?" Then wiped off her dress.

"I'm fine," said Ida. "They think they can intimidate us?"

"This is happening all over the place. That's their plan. The opposing groups are trying to convince pro-Suffrage women that it will impact them in a bad way."

A small group of women approached Kathryn. One spoke for the group. "We aren't worried about their threats," she said. "The more they shout, the more people want to join the Movement."

Rose stepped forward. You've come to the right place. Ida here has a women's club."

"Perhaps we can join you."

Ida and the woman exchanged information.

The protest lasted the rest of the afternoon and continued to grow as more people joined them.

CHAPTER NINETEEN

July 1915

The Park and the Hill

Mary and Kathryn took a walk down Main Street toward the park with their parasols on the pleasant mid-afternoon in July.

"I appreciate these walks," said Kathryn. "They help strengthen my leg and it's nice to get out on a day when it's not too hot."

When they reached the park, they went across the open grassy area.

"Sara Bard Field will be in town in two months," said Mary. "She's gathering signatures on a petition to present to Congress."

"I heard. We have to get busy. It won't be easy. I'm so glad we're on her stop. I wonder if Ida could get her to speak to the Women's Club."

"She will try. Ida said that would be a good opportunity for signatures. So maybe."

As they headed toward a shady area, Mary looked around as if searching for something. She stopped and stood on her tiptoes while leaning against a park bench.

"What is it?" Kathryn asked.

"Anna said she might meet me here. She's thinking of abandoning the Suffrage Movement. I want to talk to her."

"Why would she abandon it?"

"She's been questioning it for some time."

"I wondered, with her absences from the meetings."

Kathryn was about to sit until Mary said, "Isn't that Rose? It looks like she's crying."

"Let's go," Kathryn said.

"Maybe she wants to be alone. Should we?"

"Yes, let's go."

They went across the park grounds to a bench where Rose was sitting at the far end, leaning forward into her handkerchief.

Mary kneeled next to her. "Rose, what is upsetting you?"

Kathryn sat next to her.

"John and I had a fight," Rose said. "This is where we usually go to make up, but he went out fishing with Alan Stephens."

"Do you want—?" Kathryn began.

"—you don't have to tell us anything, Rose," Mary said.

"I mean," Kathryn said, "do you want company, because we'd be happy to take you downtown to the new soda shop."

"I'd like that."

They stood. Mary and Kathryn locked arms with Rose and they all headed up Main to the soda fountain at Frazier's Pharmacy.

"Oh my!" said Rose as they stepped in. "What a fancy new place. Look at those swivel stools along the counter."

Three smiling attendants stood behind the counter. Kathryn, Mary and Rose sat at the counter and as they were about to place an order, Violette Stephens walked in. They invited her to sit with them. Rose tried to maintain a pleasant demeanor.

"Hello there," Violette said. "I'm glad I ran into you all with Alan busy."

They invited Violette to join them.

"What's Alan up to?" asked Kathryn.

"He was going fishing, but his plans got changed, so he's home."

Meanwhile

Beneath the cottonwood trees, a refreshing breeze wafted across the Promontory, sending Anna's hair floating out. She gathered it and sat back against John Shane who wrapped his arms around her.

"The view is so lovely up here," she said.

"Not as lovely as you, my sweet."

"That sounds so phony," she said with a chuckle.

"It's nice up here during the day, isn't it?"

"Much nicer," she said. "How is your Saturday going? Have you caught any fish yet?"

John laughed. "I caught me a big one."

"Oh? What about that other one? Are you going to throw her back?"

"Well, I might keep her for a while."

"I know you don't want to go through all that, but I would love to be Mrs. John Shane. Wouldn't you like that?"

"More than anything."

"I'll wait for you," she said, "but for how long?"

"Let's stay as we are for now," he said. "I'll work on it."

"You said that a month ago. I want us to be married."

"I'll take care of you until then and help you with your expenses and other things. After all, once we're married, you'll be taking care of our home and you'll be able to minimize some of your group activities."

"I'm already doing that to be with you more. I've been flexible to adapt to your schedule so we don't impact Rose and she doesn't find out."

"As I take care of you, you don't have to worry about trivial matters, things most women should leave to men, anyway."

"Well, you're very generous, dear." Anna looked out at the rolling green hills and sighed. "All that rain this summer has really kept everything green. I love the shadows the hills cast this time of day."

Shane gazed out. "Well then," he said, pulling out his pocket watch. "The day's getting on."

"What time is it now?" she asked.

"Time to start back down the hill."

"Are you supposed to take a catch home?"

"No, you can't come home with me. Not yet."

She poked an index finger into his cheek. "You haven't caught me yet, John Shane. You know what you have to do."

Shane threw his arms around her and pulled her toward him, knocking both of them off balance.

He scrambled up and said, "And you know what you have to do, or not do, as well. Rose is interested in that Suffrage stuff."

"I'm still thinking about it and if you want me, you get all of me."

"Are you planning to join a Women's Cub?"

"I might if they'll have me."

"I prefer you don't. If I'm going to leave her after twelve years, I don't want another Rose."

It'll keep me on top of their goings on."

"Maybe it will, but don't you go picking up their crazy ideas. I can do the thinking for both of us."

She patted his shoulder. "Of course you can."

CHAPTER TWENTY

Late August 1915

Photographer's Studio, Wichita

"Getting a portrait done for Christmas is a nice idea, don't you think?" John Shane said as he led Rose by the hand into the photographer's studio in a large foursquare home to a bench that faced a tripod-mounted camera. The photographer stepped behind the camera where he made some adjustments and gestured to a scene draped behind the bench. "I chose this background for you," he said. "I think an image of Venice behind you is romantic."

"Unquestionably," John said as they sat. "Don't you think, Rosie dear?"

"I think so, too," she said.

"Very well," said the photographer. He stepped toward them and reached toward John's vest. "Please permit me to do an adjustment."

"Of course."

The photographer pulled on John's watch chain to even it up.

"Oh, I'm sorry, Rosie, I thought I had that right, but I must have been careless."

"That's all right. I noticed it just as we got ready to leave, but I was so busy, I didn't mention it when you went to finish up in front of the mirror. I'm glad we have an astute photographer."

The photographer nodded his thanks and adjusted Rose's dress then went behind the camera and donned the hood.

"Beautiful," he said after taking one picture.

"She certainly is," John said, putting his arm around her shoulder.

"Careful, please," the photographer said, "I'm taking another shot."

"My apologies," John said, winking at Rose. "Sometimes I can't help myself."

"Think nothing of it," she said with little emotion.

The photographer took another shot. He pulled the plate from the camera and took it and the other one to a side room.

"Aren't you so charming?" Rose said.

"Can't I show affection with my wife outside the home?"

"A balance is usually nice."

The photographer emerged and said, "Mr. and Mrs. Shane, everything is in order. Should be ready by mid-November. Shall I arrange delivery to you in Sycamore Falls by courier?"

"It would be nice to have them delivered, don't you think, John?" suggested Rose.

"No, I'll drive over here and pick them up," John said to her. "I'll use that opportunity to take the car to the dealer where I bought it and have them service it. It'll take most of the day."

CHAPTER TWENTY-ONE

Early September 1915

Trailing Up Sugar Loaf

"I'm so glad Mr. Markley is allowing us to climb up Sugar Loaf," said Kathryn. "How did you persuade him, George?"

"He still opposes Suffrage, and his disallowing us access back when he found out about our Suffrage activities was completely unreasonable and perhaps even childish, but this is a welcomed start for him getting more friendly with all of us regardless of our efforts."

"Did your membership to the Prairie Room Club have anything to do with it?"

"It absolutely did. And they held a NAOWS meeting there one time while I was there."

"They tricked you," said Mary.

"So they think."

"Kathryn? Ready?" Rose asked.

"I'm ready—let's go."

The climb was difficult for Kathryn when they reached uneven terrain and it took a while to get up to the Promontory. When they reached the boulders beneath it, she prepared to scale them.

The others helped Kathryn over the rocks and slid onto the Promontory ledge.

"Oh, the view!" Kathryn said, looking out at the nearby hilltops that reached a little higher than here.

She crawled across the flat area under the trees.

"You did it, Kathryn! I'm so glad," said Mary.

"And, Rose," Kathryn said, "I'm sure all this isn't what you expected on what should be a leisurely walk."

Rose laughed and patted Kathryn on the shoulder.

Kathryn gazed out. "Look down in that line of trees. There's an owl."

"Ohhh," said Mary, "it's looking right at us."

"The owl can see us better than we can see it," said George. "It probably knows everything that happens up here. The stories it could tell with people coming here over the years. There's an old campfire ring of stones over there. I didn't find anything else when I first saw it so I couldn't begin to guess who camped here whenever it was long ago."

Mary decided to have a look, got on her hands and knees, and combed through the grass. After a minute or two, she found something and held it up. "Look, part of a chain."

"Let's see," said Rose.

Mary handed it to her.

"Why, that's just like John's watch chain," she said. "I thought his watch chain looked odd that day at the photographer's."

"George, do you know if John trails up here?" Kathryn asked.

"I don't know if he does much trailing, but I can imagine with his association with Mr. Markley and Miller that he could have come up here a time or two."

"You keep it, Rose," Mary said. "Maybe you can fix it if it's his."

Rose took the chain fragment and tucked it away.

Kathryn sighed. "I could stay up here for hours." She tried to peer around the tree trunk and glimpse the top of Sugar Loaf. To get a better view, she started to scoot around the trunk.

"Ouch! Oh that hurts. Something stuck me."

"Kathryn! What's wrong?" Mary said. She and Rose slid over to her.

George offered his hand. "Did you get bit or stung?"

Mary tried to get a view of the injury and George looked away.

"There it is," said Mary. Sliding the skirt aside from her hip, she said, "A tiny puncture wound. A rattlesnake bite usually has two. Maybe you sat on a sticker."

Kathryn reached down and rubbed the sore. "Don't touch it," Mary said. She reached into her pouch and retrieved a three-inch brown bottle with skull and crossbones embossed near the top with "POISON, LIQ. IODINE" below that.

"Now," she said, "grit your teeth, Kathryn, as this will sting."

It did. "I guess it's fortunate to hike with a student of nursing, isn't it?" Kathryn said.

Mary smiled and nodded. "I always carry this."

Kathryn looked at the spot on the ground where she got stuck, combed through the grass and found a small object. She didn't say what it was and carefully closed her fingers around it and tucked it away in her handkerchief.

CHAPTER TWENTY-TWO

September 1915

Sara's Visit and a Realization

Anna saw a small crowd gathered around someone on the courthouse lawn and headed straight for them. When she got closer, she saw they were waiting to greet Sara Bard Field. The crowd of mostly women included a few men and Mr. and Mrs. Markley there signing Sara Bard Field's petition. Anna found her way over there and signed it. The Markleys exited the area quickly. Anna headed across the street and decided to walk home the long way, past houses of all sizes and trees lining the streets. The fall colors were barely starting to show.

She thought as she walked.

Do I trust John? Will he be the sweet, charming man he is now if he divorces his wife and marries me? He seems too good to be true. Like that sap in Topeka. I have to start wising up to these dashing men who sweep me off my feet. And what was that bit about him doing the thinking for both of us? And him not wanting me joining a Women's Club?

I meant what I said about getting all of me. I have a good mind. He doesn't appreciate that. He's not a good man. And I'm no better. Not only that, I can't marry him and expect to change him afterwards.

And if he cheats on her with me, will he do the same to me? I have to break this off.

Anna reached her street and passed by her boarding house. More walking for thinking was good. She decided to head back to Main Street.

* * *

Kathryn shelved some books and Mary walked in. "Ida's book club meeting starts this evening," she said. "Shall we go up together?"

Kathryn finished the arrangement and went to the checkout counter. "Yes, let's go up from here. Now I want to show you something." She opened a drawer and pulled the item from its hidden place in the back.

Mary came around to that side and peered down at Kathryn's hand.

"Ohhh!" Mary said when Kathryn showed her an earring.

"Look familiar?" said Kathryn.

"Is that what stuck you on the Promontory? That's Anna's."

"It sure is."

"I never would have thought," she said.

"I did. This and John's watch chain up there. I've often wondered about her."

"Now, she's not really a bad person."

The shop door opened and Kathryn hid the earring in the back of the drawer.

Speaking of whom, Kathryn thought.

"Hello, Anna," said Mary with a smile.

"I'm looking for a book," said Anna, glancing about.

"We have lots of books here," Kathryn said.

Mary shot a disapproving glance at Kathryn.

Anna chuckled. "Well, of course. May I look around?"

"Be our guest," said Mary.

After a few minutes, she paused during her browsing. "I'm reconsidering Women's Suffrage," she said.

"What is bringing you back around?" Kathryn said.

"I am observing some people's behavior against Suffrage, some of it for questionable reasons."

"That's certainly true," said Mary.

"I would like to join Ida's Women's Group if she'll have me."

"I think she would," Kathryn said.

"Sara Bard Field is in town today," Anna said. "I signed her petition."

"That's wonderful," Mary said.

"Is there a meeting at Ida's tonight?" asked Anna.

"There is," replied Kathryn. "Would you like to go with Mary and me?"

"She has a good group. Margarete, us two, Florence, and several others," said Mary.

"And Rose Shane. She joined a couple of years ago and hadn't been for a while, but she's been back lately," Kathryn said.

"Rose, too?" Anna said. "Sounds like there's a good group. I'd love to go there with you all. Shall I meet you here at the bookshop?" Anna smiled and left the shop.

"Well," Kathryn said. "She didn't even react to hearing Rose would be there!"

"Maybe we got it wrong about her," said Mary.

"But that's definitely her earring and that was John's watch chain. I'll get the earring out before we leave for the meeting with her."

* * *

Rose was already in Ida's living room when Kathryn, Anna, and Mary arrived. Anna chose a chair next to Rose.

Ida began. "First, we have a new member. Everyone, meet Anna."

Several women smiled as they welcomed her, then a few exchanged nervous glances.

Several of them knew Anna from years before, but Kathryn didn't think she and Rose had met.

"Welcome to the group, Anna," said Rose with a smile. "Since you're new, perhaps we can get together for tea and get to know one another."

Kathryn watched every nuance in Anna's reaction. She didn't show any emotion.

"Yes," said Anna, "I would like that."

"It's settled then. My residence Sunday afternoon. Mr. Shane will be out and we ladies will have the house to ourselves."

Anna seemed tickled at the idea. "Sounds lovely!"

Ida changed the subject. "I have good news for this great turnout. At the close of the meeting, Sara Bard Field will join us briefly with her petition to sign before she heads on to Washington in the car."

"Good news, indeed!" said Margarete.

"Kathryn," said Ida, "I understand you've achieved some success in your quest to climb Sugar Loaf."

"With help from my trailing companions," Kathryn said.

"Kathryn, dear, don't minimize your accomplishments. With your bad leg, you've overcome something that seemed improbable before. It's all right to reach your goal with the help of others."

CHAPTER TWENTY-THREE

September 1915

Anna's Visit

Main Street was busy with traffic on this sunny early afternoon in September as Anna walked along the storefronts. She came to East Fourth Street and turned down it. Yellow leaves sailed in light breezes as she strode among the tall elm trees that lined the street.

After a couple of blocks, she came to a recently built house. Its roof sloped from the roofline to the front, forming the porch overhang.

Rose answered the door.

"I love the style of your home," said Anna.

"It's called American Craftsman, a new style."

She led Anna into a spacious living room and invited her to sit in one of the wingback chairs next to the windows. A butler's table in front of the chairs held a china teapot, matching creamer, sugar bowl with cups and saucers, and a plate of cookies.

Rose held up the creamer. "Do you take cream in your tea?"

"Yes, please."

She poured a dollop into a cup and added tea to it then handed Anna the cup and a little plate, and sat in the chair next to her.

"John's out this afternoon," said Rose. "I don't always know where he goes on Sunday afternoons; sometimes I think to his office or that Prairie Room Club."

Anna felt a pain at the pit of her stomach for *she* knew where he went, and she wouldn't be there to meet him. She leaned over to let the breeze from the open windows brush against her face then she focused on her host.

Rose took a sip from her cup. "Wasn't it nice to meet Sara Bard Field on her stop here? She's driving all the way from California to Washington, DC, collecting signatures on that petition. We'll win this, Anna!"

Anna chuckled and they stood and shook hands.

"I was part of the Movement a while back but left it," Anna said.

"What brought you back?"

"A gentleman friend who I thought was in favor of it revealed his true feelings. He displayed what I think many who oppose Suffrage are thinking. And he told me I am too pretty to need the vote. Can you imagine?"

"That's all too common. We have to keep moving forward, Anna."

"Yes, we're all in this together."

"I'm so glad we met," said Rose.

"Oh, so am I."

"Aren't you new in town?"

"I was born and raised in Sycamore Falls, but after I got married, we moved to Topeka. He left me and I moved back here."

"I'm sorry that happened to you, Anna. Perhaps you'll meet someone new."

Anna held back tears. "Thank you," she said. "I had someone, but I am breaking it off and won't see him anymore."

Rose took a deep breath. "Is it John, my husband?" she asked quietly.

"Rose, I am so sorry. Yes it is—*was!*—I was lonely and he was kind. I didn't know he was married at first. I feel so foolish and terrible for you. I should never—"

"I know well about the Shane charm," said Rose. "I suspect you're not the only one. He and I are on our way out." It almost appeared to Anna that a weight was lifted from Rose's shoulders. Rose reached over and held Anna's arm. "We're like sisters, Anna."

"Yes—thank you."

"The Suffrage fight will continue, too. Welcome back."

A car pulled up.

"Well, there he is now," said Rose.

"I was supposed to meet him," said Anna.

"I would love to hide you and see what he says about why he's back so soon, but maybe we should just act as normal.

John came in the front door and displayed little emotion as he entered the living room.

"Miller was supposed to meet me this afternoon to discuss how to deal with this Woman Suffrage nonsense and talk investments," he said, "but I'm glad he didn't show up with what Reverend Bruce says about working on Sunday." He glanced at Anna. "Oh, how do you do? I am John."

"I asked Anna over for tea," Rose said.

"Glad to know you," John said.

"Hello, John, sorry I didn't meet you," Anna said with a smirk. "Rose knows about us but I'm through with you."

After a few moments of subdued tension, John headed to the kitchen.

After he left the room, Anna and Rose tried to keep their laughter quiet, but a few snickers came out.

"Rose," Anna said, "I should leave now. Thank you for a lovely time."

"It was enlightening," Rose said.

"Yes!"

Anna headed to the door and left the Shane residence. She walked down Fourth Street and after a block, she thought she heard something behind her. A glance back revealed nothing so she continued on her way to downtown and went up Main Street to the gazebo on the courthouse lawn.

She didn't know what to think as she mulled things over:

Should we have confronted John like that? That *was* fun. He deceived both of us, and I don't like his attitude about women. Now that I'm getting to know Rose a little, I'm so ashamed of the whole affair. By the time I knew he was married, I let my emotions rule and I know I should have broken it off then. Yet I kept on with him, susceptible to his promises and charm, but that's no excuse for breaking up their marriage. After all, I suffered the same fate in Topeka and now I was going to do that to someone else? A big mistake. I hope Rose forgives me. She seems to. How does John treat her? She said they were on their way out, but maybe they could have worked out their differences, I don't know. I'm glad I'm doing the right thing now and never meeting him again. Goodbye, fancy lifestyle. I'm so lonely. People tell me I'm pretty, but I'm more than that. I know I am more. I want the other women to like me, too. And for men to like me for me, not for my pretty face. Kathryn's pretty, too, but she's respected for her accomplishments and she is doing amazing things with her trailing. I don't envy her that leg problem. She persists and reaches her goals.

Anna sighed and kept thinking.

Maybe getting involved in Ida's clubs will be nice. Suffrage must be worth the effort so many are putting in.

A fancy car speeding down Main interrupted her thoughts as it tore around a corner.

John.

She reached for her small purse and discovered she didn't have it and must have left it at the Shane house. She didn't want to see John again, but could pay Rose another visit maybe before he got back home. She trudged down Main Street toward Rose's street, thinking:

Rose and I can be really good friends. Never before have I had "girlfriends." Always a loner except for men around sometimes, falling over each other for my attention, but no real friendships. This could be a new start for me. If John doesn't cause trouble, then Rose and I can meet for things around town.

She reached Rose's street and approached the Shane residence, went to the front door. No one was home, but the door was ajar. She peeked in, saw her purse, ran in, and grabbed it. There was a small spill on the floor next to her chair. She felt embarrassed that she might have accidently caused that when she and Rose were laughing about their situation. She felt anxious and rushed back onto the porch and left.

CHAPTER TWENTY-FOUR

September 1915

A Country Road Outside of Sycamore Falls

On this warm September day, things had mostly dried up from the rain. The leaves in the foliage canopy were just starting to change.

Rose made it this far along the road and needed to find a good way through the woods toward that ranch house. After another half hour walk, she finally found a good way, squeezed between the wooden fence's horizontal poles, and went into the woods. She knew about snakes and took care to avoid stepping in the wrong places the wrong way, but this way was her best option. In a couple more months, most snakes would be hibernating.

She continued through the woods, away from the road, avoiding being seen by going this way, going downhill, skipping over small outcrops and reached what she assumed was a tributary to Elm River. It was too wide and deep to get across so she walked along its bank, rounding uprooted trees lying on their sides that leaned out across the creek. She wouldn't attempt using one as a bridge. Maybe if she were twelve again. But it was getting pretty warm now and the foliage above wasn't cooling

much. She removed her hat and fanned her face as she left the last of the downed trees behind.

She finally got to a shallower part of the creek. If she could get down to the water, she could cool off. After a few bends in the creek, she arrived at a possible way down. The creek curved more here. The wide rocky area where the stream's flow had deposited stones over time provided a good place to access the water. She just needed to get to it. She found a place to climb down the earthen bank to the rocky area and went to the water's edge where she knelt and cupped her hand in the flow then brought the cooling water to the wound on her face which refreshed her and helped divert her attention from the pain in her shoulder and upper arm. She rested here in the cool of the creek for a while and wrung out the hem of her dress.

She could see prairie beyond the tree trunks across the creek and waded across, never mind ruining her shoes, reached the far bank, clambered up, and started walking through the remaining woods toward the open prairie. She figured she must be close and resisted the urge to hurry. She had to maneuver around bushy undergrowth, managing to avoid stickers and went by several blackberry bushes at which she stopped a time or two for a treat before continuing to the open prairie.

She emerged from the woods, waded through the tallgrass, and from a small rise could see all around. There it was ahead on a small hill, a fancy ranch house with a wooden fence. There was no car next to it. Maybe the lady was home alone.

Rose made her way to the house and Clara Markley greeted her at the door.

"Rose! Come in and sit down at once! What happened!"

Clara led Rose into the living room to a comfortable chair.

Rose sighed and started crying. "John beat me!"

"Oh, lord! Just a moment, let me get something for that wound."

Clara retrieved a soapy damp cloth and looked closely at the injury. She patted Rose's face with the cloth and applied some coal tar powder to the wound and started to pat Rose's shoulder until Rose jerked it away. "Your shoulder, too?"

"Yes!"

"Why did he do this to you?"

"We argued about women voting and I also confronted him about his affairs and it led to a terrible fight then—"

"There, there, you don't have to talk about it. Let's take care of you now and I think Doc Hall should see you."

"No, I'll be fine. I don't want this to get around."

"You did nothing to deserve this."

"But people might think I did and blame me and he might get others to believe him."

"You stay here and rest until Fred gets home. I'll send him into town to fetch Doc Hall."

"Should Mr. Markley see me like this and have him know about what happened? He and John are friends."

"Don't you worry about it. Fred's a reasonable man."

She led Rose to a small bedroom and had her lie down. Clara opened the windows and a gentle gust sent the curtains floating in and the breeze across Rose's face calmed her.

"You rest and I'll get some things done. Shout if you need anything."

"Thank you, Mrs. Markley."

Clara stepped out of the room, easing the door closed. All was quiet now with only the sounds of prairie insects and breezes outside. The small gusts died down for a while and all was still. Rose closed her eyes and the violence replayed, but she wanted to relax and tried not think of it. It was hard. She tossed everything around in her mind: Anna, John, Women's Club, Suffrage. Was Suffrage worth it? The struggle? Could she just go on as before and be happy without it? No—that's what those who opposed it wanted her to think. She had friends now since joining the club, unlike before, with few acquaintances.

She finally dozed to the subdued singing of the insects and the refreshing breeze.

* * *

She stirred awake. Oh dear! Did it really happen? Her face and shoulder still hurt. She sighed and decided to lie there for a while longer. The sound of a car pulling up followed by footsteps signaled Mr. Markley's arrival. Rose overheard Clara and him engaged in subdued conversation in the living room.

"He what!"

"Shh!"

"Then we'll see about that. Of course I'll go get Doc Hall."

He left and Rose got up and went to open the bedroom door.

Clara served tea and she and Rose spent the next hour sitting on the sofa near the window that had a view of the Markley land. Rose gazed out at the woods in the distance that she traipsed though to get here. Beyond the treetops stood Sugar Loaf.

"I walked partway up that hill with Kathryn, Mary, and George. And do you know what we found beneath the trees on that Promontory? Why, sitting in the grass there was part of John's watch chain and do you know what else?"

"A lot of people have been up there."

"I am sure, but how many were pretty young ladies who lost an earring?"

"An earring?"

"Kathryn showed me later what she found on our hike there. None other than one of Anna's silver leaf earrings. Now why do you suppose those two items were there?"

"That Anna. I never liked her."

"I'm starting to like her though. She and I share a common bond and she's not so bad once you get to know her."

"And what a pretty lady she is," said Clara.

"She's more than that. I think she has some schooling behind her. But never mind those things. She's very repentant about her involvement with John. She said she's not going to see him anymore."

"See that she doesn't if you want him back."

"I'm afraid of him and I don't want him back. He has hurt me before. Not this badly, but it's something he's done from time to time. I missed church for a couple of weeks last fall because I had a black eye."

"All right, Rose, from now on, as long as you're with him—anyone—you come to me at once if you get hurt like you did today, do you understand? But try to get a ride out here."

Rose nodded and looked into her teacup as she carefully swirled it. "I will. I cannot tell you how much I appreciate your help, Mrs. Markley."

"Call me Clara, please." She looked out the window. "Uh oh. Get down, Rose." Clara stood and stepped away from the window.

"What is it?"

"Just stay low and go back to the bedroom."

Rose complied, pulling the bedroom door in, and as Clara went to answer a knock at the door, Rose peered out.

John's voice.

"No, said Clara shaking her head. "I haven't seen her since church."

John said something.

"Sorry, no. I'm not feeling well. Doc Hall is coming to check on me soon and he said it might be something catching. You best run along and stay clear. Yes, Fred will be at the Prairie Room Club tomorrow evening. You can see him then."

John mumbled something and left.

Rose sighed in relief and emerged from the bedroom.

Clara gestured to a chair away from the window and Rose sat.

"What did he want?" asked Rose.

"He's looking for you."

"I shouldn't be surprised. It'll be time for his supper soon."

"He can go downtown and eat," said Clara, "or find something at home. He won't starve."

Rose jumped when the door opened.

"There she is," said Markley as he and Doc Hall entered.

Doc went to Rose and knelt next to her. He looked closely at her facial wound and examined her eyes, then took her pulse. "Pulse is normal. Fred says you applied coal tar, Mrs. Markley. You did the right thing." He turned to Rose. "I want to see you if you develop a fever in case of blood poisoning."

"I will send for you," she said.

He looked into her eyes. "Any dizziness or confusion?"

"No."

He gently touched her arm and shoulder and she flinched. "Doesn't look like anything's broken, but your shoulder and upper arm will be sore for a bit," he said.

"I want you to stay here for a few days," Clara said. "You can sleep in that second bedroom where you were."

"I second that," said Fred.

"If I may," said Doc Hall, "it'd be good for you to accept the Markleys' hospitality, rest here and not be doing chores."

Rose sighed. "Very well, but if I wear out my welcome, Clara, you tell me right away."

Meanwhile

Anna, Mary, and Kathryn walked down Main Street toward Fourth Street and headed toward the Shane house.

"And if John is there, what then?" asked Anna.

"Nothing," replied Kathryn. "We're looking for Rose, nothing more."

"Not that we can't handle John," said Mary "but I'm glad you're with us, Kathryn."

They continued along the street and reached the craftsman-style house. A Packard sat out front.

"He's home," said Anna.

They walked up to the front door and knocked.

John answered. "Well now, it's not often I'm visited by three beauties."

"We're here to see Rose," Kathryn said.

"She's not home."

"Where'd she go?" Kathryn insisted.

Shane shrugged. "I don't know. She left a few hours ago and hasn't been back. She didn't say where she was going."

"How was she feeling?" asked Mary.

Shane smiled. "Fine. Jovial."

"All right, fine," said Anna, "let's go, girls."

The three of them turned and headed down the porch steps as Shane bowed sarcastically and went back inside.

"I don't trust him," said Anna. "Rose *was* in jovial spirits when I left here earlier, but I heard something when I walked away, like shouting. I didn't see her leave the house, so I don't know." Anna looked down and stopped for a moment.

"What's wrong, Anna?" said Mary.

"If anything's happened to Rose, I feel responsible."

"No!" said both Kathryn and Mary.

"If anything's happened, it's probably John's doing, Anna" said Kathryn.

"We need to look for her," said Mary.

"John told me before that she goes to the park to 'sulk' as he put it," said Anna.

"Oh, brother," said Kathryn. "Well, let's go. We found her there once after a fight with John, Anna. Perhaps."

They went to the park and searched all around it for Rose but found no trace of her."

The Road to Sugar Loaf: A Suffragist's Story

"The day's getting on," said Kathryn, glancing west through the trees at the sunset. "Rose would normally be home now."

CHAPTER TWENTY-FIVE

September 1915

Prairie Room Club and Doc

George leaned against the bookshop checkout counter. "I ran into John Shane on Main Street today. He insists he doesn't know where Rose is."

"He's lying," said Kathryn.

Mary nodded.

"Mr. Markley invited me to meet him at the Prairie Room Club in a little while."

"Is he going to keep inviting you again to join?"

"I don't know. He didn't seem to be in that kind of mood." George drummed his fingers on the counter. "I'm going to urge him to get on John to try to determine where Rose is and what's going on."

"Good luck to him and you," said Kathryn.

"I agree," said Mary.

George looked at his watch. "I need to leave soon," he said.

"Whatever you can say to convince him to really press John Shane, even if it jeopardizes our access to the hill," reiterated Kathryn.

"I'll do my best."

* * *

In the Prairie Room Club, Theodore Miller took a seat in a chair next to Markley and pulled out a cigar. "What have you got for me, Fred? You seemed urgent."

Markley leaned forward. "That little sap, John Shane beat his wife."

"What!" Miller said. "How do you know? That cute little gal?"

"She's hurt, staying with us, and Doc Hall had to come out and see her."

"Doc Hall? I was just in his office this morning. He didn't say anything about it."

"He won't. I'm only telling you so you know what kind of man John Shane is and that we might need to expel him from here."

"But what caused it? Did she do something? She must have."

"I don't know, but nothing she could've done deserved what I saw."

"That bad?"

"Bad."

Miller sat back. "There's got to be an explanation. I know him. He wouldn't do something like that unless provoked. She's gotten involved with those 'Suffragettes'. They're nothing but trouble and if they get what they want, mark my words, divorce rates will go up faster than you can shake a stick. This is only the beginning of the destruction of the role of the sexes." He held out his cigar for a light.

Markley ignored the gesture. "Whatever she thinks along those lines, she's entitled to her beliefs."

"Do you really believe that? What about Mrs. Markley?"

Markley harrumphed. "Mrs. Markley and I are happy. I'll insist you not presume to question our relationship."

Miller stood and left without excusing himself and George walked in.

"Have a seat, my boy, but be careful, that chair has a stench of close-mindedness."

George looked confused.

Markley chuckled. "Never mind. I want to tell you about Rose Shane. She's safe."

"Thank God."

"John Shane beat her something awful."

"I was afraid it was something terrible. We need to tell the others, they're very worried."

"She's staying with us at the ranch. Mrs. Markley is caring for her. I'll leave it to you to tell the ladies."

"They'll surely want to visit her."

"Of course, but let me check with Rose and Mrs. Markley first."

"Then I'll wait to hear from you."

"I'll send word over to your school."

George remained when John Shane walked into the club.

"Rose is missing," Shane said as he sat next to them.

"She's at our place," Markley said.

"Why?"

"You beat her so bad she needs care."

"From an argument and a little slap?"

"If she doesn't get better soon, I'm having you arrested."

"For one little marriage quarrel? You exaggerate. I'm coming out to your place to see her."

"You're not setting foot on our property."

"So Clara wasn't really ill yesterday when I went by. You're obligated to let me see my wife."

"No I'm not."

"I'll send the sheriff out," Shane insisted.

"He'll see Rose's injuries," Markley said.

"You won't get away with this."

"Nor will you," said George.

"Go put a skirt on, Fielding," Shane said.

George laughed. "I can't find a style I like that fits."

Markley chuckled. "Well, George," he said, "perhaps you'll consider joining the club here in Shane's stead since his days here are numbered."

Shane got up and stormed out.

Markley chuckled and muttered, "Can't find a style you like that fits. Heh heh heh."

"One of my students drew a picture on the blackboard a couple of years ago of me wearing a dress as a commentary on my support of Women's Suffrage."

"Well, I'm feeling a bit better about it these days. Shane and Miller demonstrate why it just might have merit. There are other things as well. Mrs. Markley has been in support of it since before it passed in Kansas."

George nodded. "I began to understand when I was trailing on your land a few years ago near those ruins in the woods."

"Now that's interesting, because that was our home when I was a youngin."

"Sometime you might tell me a little about those days."

"It was hard times for us since we were just starting out. Things were especially hard for my mother trying to raise us kids. Most of the townspeople were respectful, but some men harassed her when she went into town on errands. I remember how she dreaded coming into town. I offered to go for her, but she wouldn't let me go by myself until I got a little older. My dad got on me a lot because I often moped around that nice land worrying about little Indian kids who had to leave their homes, but you probably don't want to hear about that."

"I *do* want to. We discuss it openly in class."

"Those days are reminders of things that make me think hard about some changes that might be upon us and how those might be changes for the better. As you can tell, I've had an inner struggle, but I can be influenced by close-minded men such as Shane and Miller and in a good way, by men like you. And I hope you help Miss Wolfe get to the top of the hill someday. I figure she struggles with that leg."

George offered his hand. Markley took it.

He stood. "Well my boy, I need to get home. I want to check on Rose and I want to get out there in case Shane decides to show up uninvited." Markley went to the exit then said, "I'll find out about Rose receiving visitors and let you know."

Markley went to his new Dodge automobile and drove down Main Street south toward the street that led to West Hill Road. He appreciated the good handling of this car as he drove along the moderately curvy country road. He had to be careful on unpaved roads like West Hill. A lot ran through his mind as he rounded curves. He sped up when approaching hills so he'd make it up them without having to stop and turn the car around and go up backwards. He wondered who thought of putting the fuel tank under the seat in this car and other makes. That was senseless.

When he reached the base of the last hill before his turn off, he sped along the mostly straight road. He didn't slow down enough for one of the hill's rock-lined bumps. The jolt sent the car sideways onto its side. Unhurt, he avoided panic and pulled himself out onto the gravel. He felt lucky to be alive and while disheartened to see his new car on its side, but he worried more about Rose.

He stood, brushed himself off, turned to walk up the hill. He would have to ride Daisy into town for help.

A horn from behind startled him: a Packard pulled up, stopping behind the wreck and John Shane hopped out.

"Are you all right!" he shouted.

Markley went to face him. "Just shaken up a little. In better shape than my car."

"You're in a little predicament, aren't you?"

"I'll manage."

"If you promise not to expel me and back me up if I have trouble with Rose, I'll take you into town and help you get this taken care of."

"I'll leave it to you to let the sheriff know about the wreck blocking the road," said Markley. "About Rose and not expelling you, no deal."

"Suit yourself, Markley." Shane went back to his car, sped away.

Markley got to his ranch house and Clara greeted him.

"How is Rose?" he asked.

"Not well. Go see her."

Clara followed and Markley stepped up to the bed. Rose lay there with a cool cloth on her head.

"She's got a fever," said Clara.

"How bad?"

"She feels hot, but hopefully it's a mild one."

Markley felt her forehead. "We need to get Doc back out." He told Clara about the accident and said he'd be riding Daisy into town.

Rose stirred awake.

Tell me how you feel," he said.

"I was fine this morning, then by afternoon, I felt a achy and got this fever."

"I'll go get Doc Hall."

"I think I'll be fine with a little rest."

Clara shook her head. "Nonsense, dear. Doc will help you feel better."

Markley saddled up Daisy and rode into town, first to see Doc Hall, then to the sheriff's office to report his accident.

Back at the Markley ranch, Markley and Doc entered the living room.

Doc went to Rose, closed the door and after a few minutes emerged back into the living room.

"She's quite sick. I'm afraid she's got blood poisoning. Give her two of these aspirin tablets." He pulled a clear bottle with "Bayer" embossed on the front out of his bag and handed it to Clara.

"Will she be all right?" she asked Doc.

"She should survive it. She needs a lot of water even if she's not thirsty. I'll be back out tomorrow."

* * *

Markley spent the next day taking care of the wreck. It was fortunate that Newman's Gas Company had a service truck with an auto crane and was able to go out, pull the Dodge upright, and tow it into their station in Sycamore Falls which freed up Markley to keep tabs on Rose. He rode out with Doc and waited in the living room with Clara.

"Her temperature is still high," Doc said. "I'm making hospital arrangements in Wichita. I just got the word this morning. Alan Stephens has offered to drive Rose over and you both can ride with us if you wish. Rose isn't contagious so she won't be in an isolation ward."

Later, Doc Hall, Fred, and Clara helped Rose into Alan's car, and they headed to Wichita as Clara comforted Rose along the way.

A few hours later, in late evening, Alan dropped the Markleys off at their ranch.

"Dr. Powers in Wichita will keep me updated on her condition," said Doc as they left.

* * *

A day later, the Women's Club convened on Ida's porch.

"I wish we could have seen Rose before she was taken to the hospital in Wichita," said Kathryn. "Doc Hall said they had to get her there quickly. I can't concentrate on work worrying about her."

"Anna has been moping around, too," said Mary, suppressing a cry.

Margarete arrived a few minutes later. "Doc Hall got an update," she said. "They've decided on treatment. There are some promising new antimicrobials to help her fight this."

"Oh, thank God," said Mary.

"I have an idea," said Ida. "We should find out if Rose can have visitors."

"A wonderful idea," said Mary.

"We could take the train or see if someone can drive us over," said Kathryn.

"I'll find out about visitors," said Ida.

Kathryn glanced at Margarete. "What do you have, Margarete?"

Margarete showed them the latest issue of *Woman's World and Suffrage News*.

"Any news? We could use a diversion for a moment," said Kathryn.

Margarete held it up. "It says here that Carrie Chapman Catt now supports a national amendment to grant Women's Suffrage and she no longer says we should gain the vote through individual states first to elect a pro-Suffrage majority in Congress."

"Good, because that would take longer," said Kathryn. "There's no guarantee women would elect enough pro-Suffrage senators and representatives to override a presidential veto if we have an anti-Suffrage president. I'm glad she's finally coming around."

Mary sighed and gazed out at the view. "After Rose gets better, we should make plans to walk up Sugar Loaf again, Kathryn, if Mr. Markley will allow it."

"I think he will. Have I told you all what George said? That Mr. Markley has warmed up to him and is even getting more accepting of Suffrage. I want to go back to the hill, but I can't think about that until Rose is well and comes home."

"What of John Shane?"

"I've heard that his clients are shunning him after learning what happened," said Mary.

CHAPTER TWENTY-SIX

Late September 1915

Union Station and St. Francis Hospital, Wichita

Kathryn, Mary, Anna, George, and Margarete gathered their things as their train slowed to a stop next to the boarding platform at Wichita Union Station.

"They have a Harvey's lunch and dining room," said Margarete. "We're anxious to see Rose, but shall we have lunch first?"

The rest agreed and the conductor led them off the train. They entered the cavernous concourse and started for Harvey's, their footsteps echoing throughout as they walked along the wide aisle between mostly occupied rows of seats with families, everyone dressed in their best travel clothes.

"What a big, beautiful place," said Mary gazing up and around at the high ceiling and the tall arched windows on the front side. "It's so new and so modern."

"It just opened two years ago," said Margarete.

They found Harvey's and went to the curved lunch counter.

* * *

After lunch, when they walked out in front of Union Station, Kathryn looked up at the building. "Look at those Greek columns, Mary," she said.

"It's beautiful."

Margarete pointed up the street. "Four or five blocks to Broadway where we can catch the streetcar north to St. Francis."

They boarded the northbound streetcar and squeezed their way between sign-holding women to a seat. Signs read: "We demand an amendment" and "Women Vote." Kathryn started talking to one of the banner carriers. A couple of blocks later, one woman pointed to a building entrance with a banner that read, "The Association Against a Woman's Right to Vote."

"That will be gone one day," the woman said.

A man stood and leaned toward the window. "What are you protesting?" he said to the woman. "Women got the right to vote in Kansas in 1912."

"We need more than that; we need a national amendment," she said.

The discussion only went on for a few moments.

Kathryn then noticed Mary doing some sightseeing. She glanced out the window. "Look at those big, beautiful buildings," Mary said.

"They've had a building boom here for the past fifteen years," said Kathryn.

As they continued north, the tall buildings thinned out and they reached ornate, red brick St. Francis Hospital capped with steeples.

Inside, Sister Germaine greeted them, led them to a long hallway. "Pleased to meet you all," she said. "I am Rose's nurse. "She is quite ill, but she's making progress."

She took them into a room with several women-occupied metal beds. Sister Germaine made a Shh! gesture as they entered. "Rose is awake and you may talk softly. Two others are sleeping."

Rose flashed a big smile as they approached.

Mary gasped when she saw Rose's facial wound. She knelt next to the bed and looked at Sister Germaine for approval before taking Rose's extended hand. The nurse smiled and nodded then went to sit on a corner chair.

"Rose, dear, how are you feeling?" whispered Mary.

"I'm better today, much better since you've all come. Fill me in on what's going on."

"Uh, well," began Kathryn.

"It's fine, Kathryn," said Rose. "Something about John?"

"I wasn't sure you would want to talk about him."

"Do tell. What's the gossip?"

"George?" Kathryn said to him.

"Well," started George. "it looks like John's out of the Prairie Room Club and he's losing clients."

"In fact," said Anna, "he's been scarce around town. And do you know what?"

Rose perked up and the others leaned closer.

"He came over to my home. I met him in my boarding house living room and he wants to court me. He said you and he are likely through."

"No doubt," said Rose. "Go on. . ."

"He said he is sure he can get his business going again if 'we' move to another town."

"We?" said Margarete.

Anna and Rose suppressed a laugh.

"If he doesn't end up in jail," said Margarete.

"One more thing," said Anna. "He actually asked me how much alimony I'm getting from my ex-husband in Topeka and if it's a decent amount, that maybe we could just be together and not marry so I keep the money coming in."

"I can't believe he's moving on so fast with you in the hospital," said Kathryn.

"It shows his character," said George.

Sister Germaine stood and came over to Rose's bed.

"Excuse me. It's time to check your temperature, Rose."

The others went to stand by the door and returned to Rose when the nurse was done.

"My temperature is down," said Rose.

"That's great," said Kathryn. "May I ask, was it the beating that caused the fever?"

"Indirectly. I wasn't thinking clearly and splashed creek water onto my wound and got an infection in my blood. It would have been worse if Clara hadn't applied the coal tar to it and if Doc Hall hadn't arranged to get me here so quickly."

A doctor entered. "Oh, hello, Dr. Powers," Rose said softly. She gathered the others close. "He's a heart doctor."

"Oh my," said Kathryn.

The doctor approached and the others stood back while he felt her head and used a new kind of stethoscope to listen to her chest. He and Rose spoke quietly and he stood to leave. "Ladies, and sir, that's all I needed to do. Thank you."

They went back to Rose.

"Are you all right?" asked Mary, holding Rose's hand.

"He says I am, and my heart sounds mostly fine, but he thought at first some of the infection could get to it. Now he says I might go home in a few days."

They all smiled. "That is fabulous," said Kathryn. "We miss you."

CHAPTER TWENTY-SEVEN

Early October 1915

Main Street Bookshop

Anna stepped into Main Street Bookshop with news. "Rose comes home tomorrow!"

"How wonderful!" said Kathryn.

"She's going home with John there?" asked Mary.

"No," said Anna, "she has to rest up for a while and get her strength back for a couple of months. The infection ravished her body. She'll stay at the Markley ranch where they can take care of her until after Thanksgiving. And we're all invited to their home for Thanksgiving dinner!"

"Won't that be fun!" said Mary.

"When I spoke to Mr. Markley, Anna continued, "he said we can visit her there in the meantime and Rose is welcome to stay with them as long as she needs."

"Oh my," said Kathryn, "the Markleys are saints. I never before thought I'd ever say that."

The bookshop door opened and John Shane stepped in.

Anna gasped followed by suppressed gasps from Kathryn and Mary. He fixed his gaze on Anna as the door closed behind him.

"May I help you find a book?" said Kathryn.

"No, I just found what I'm looking for." Then he glanced back at Anna, "My offer is still open, Sweet."

"Don't call me that."

"You always liked it when you wanted me to divorce Rose. Now you and I are free to have each other without sneaking about."

"The answer is, still no."

"Look what you're giving up. Do you want to be lonely and poor?"

"If I were the proprietor," said Anna, "I'd ask you to leave right now."

Kathryn drummed her fingers on the counter. "You don't have to, Anna, I will do it for you."

"I'll leave then," he said. "Looks like there's nothing for me here. At least not anymore." He turned toward the door. "You're not welcome to visit Rose when she comes home, Anna," he said as he left.

Anna sighed. "He has no idea."

"Has he ever?" said Kathryn.

"You handled that well, Anna," said Mary.

"He forgets how well I know him although that's not something of which I'm proud. I do hope you all forgive me. I still feel responsible for what happened to Rose."

"You're not!" said Kathryn.

"John is responsible for what happened," said Mary.

CHAPTER TWENTY-EIGHT

October 1915

Markley Ranch

Rose woke one October morning to rain pattering on the roof of the Markley ranch house, content as she pulled the covers tighter and rolled onto her back. She felt safe here at the Markley ranch and enjoyed the serene environment of their home out here in the hills. One of the windows was open a bit and a light breeze laced with mist wafted in. It wasn't making anything wet at all to motivate her to get up and close the window, so she lay there to think for a while.

What of my home? Do I move into a boarding home like where Anna lives? What of my things? Sell them? Some maybe but not the heirlooms. There is Mother's tea set, some of her wooden furniture like the desk Great Uncle Ralph made and Great Aunt Laura's cane chairs and the secretary desk Uncle Walter made. I would have to find somewhere safe for them. Or maybe I can get a small house, nothing like that big craftsman. It was too big for just John and me anyway. I was planning to have a baby someday, but I don't know. Will I be alone now? Maybe I should look for one of those bungalow houses that I could decorate in a nice way. And as for being alone, single women often share homes. Maybe with my new friend Anna? Or will I marry again? And what of John? What trouble will he make? But first, I need to get my physical self back to normal. Getting back into Women's Club activities would be nice and doing what I can to help the Suffrage Movement. There must be some way I can contribute although I might have to wait until I get my strength back.

Rose stretched and slid her hands under the pillow beneath her head and closed her eyes for a few minutes. She dozed for a while until someone tapped on the door.

"Good morning, Rose," said Clara. "Would you like some breakfast?"

Rose got up, dressed, and went into the kitchen. The morning sun had emerged from the last of the rain clouds and cast its brilliance onto the table where Clara had set out omelets, grapefruit, cereal, and rice cakes with maple syrup.

"You've been feeding me so well, Clara," said Rose.

"So you can build up your strength."

After breakfast, Clara invited her into the living room to relax and chat for a while. Clara picked up the copy of *Woman's World and Suffrage News* that sat on a side table.

"Well," she said, "New York has Suffrage on the ballot next month. There's thinking it has a chance of passing."

"That would be wonderful," said Rose.

"Incidentally, you must miss going to your Women's Club meetings."

"Oh, I do. I attended very few before John beat me."

"Then I should like to invite the club to meet here sometimes and bring it to you," said Clara.

Rose nearly cried with joy. "I really appreciate that!"

"I've been thinking how unfortunate it is that some people—more than we'd like—will side with John. They'll say it's his prerogative to discipline you."

"That's the cruelest discipline I've ever heard of," said Rose. "And what of his adultery?"

"You'll have more sympathy about that," assured Clara, "but you'd have to prove it to some people."

"Anna might help, although that could be bad for her. She and I are friends now."

"You two might be able to unite against John."

"If Anna agrees."

A Packard drove up and its horn sounded. Clara and Rose went to the window.

"That's John!" said Rose.

Fred Markley stepped out of the car.

"Are they friends again?" asked Rose

Clara leaned toward the window. "He's alone, Rose. It's all right."

Fred came in the front door. "Say, ladies! What do you think of my new acquisition?"

"You bought a Packard?" Clara said in a disapproving tone. "Oh, Fred."

"Don't worry. I needed a car and I got this on the cheap."

Rose laughed. "You bought John's car!"

"For a song. He needs money, so I had the advantage. Funny, he always boasted about being such a deal maker." Fred patted his heart. "Being the generous man I am, I agreed to take it off his hands for a whole seven hundred."

"Oh my," said Clara. "Rose, Fred told me they're almost six thousand dollars new."

"It's only a year old," he said. "I hope he kept it serviced well."

"That I can vouch for," said Rose. "He was truthful about most of his trips to get the car serviced. I could always tell, because he usually mumbled about the car after the servicing trips, but after the other jaunts, he babbled on and didn't give straight answers to my questions."

"You could read him like a book," said Fred.

"I do like to read and I've developed quite the reading skills."

They erupted in laughter.

Fred reached into his pocket, pulled out a small case with a bracelet. "I found this in the car," he said. "Is this yours, Rose?" He handed it to her.

She took the bracelet out.

"It's lovely," said Clara. "Look, it's engraved."

Rose inspected it. "Yes it is lovely, but it's not mine."

On the inside, the inscription read: *To Anne, My Sweet, Love John.*

CHAPTER TWENTY-NINE

November 21, 1915

Markley Ranch Visit

Anna and Rose sat next to each other on the sofa in the Markleys' living room across from George. A fire roared in the stone fireplace and a Christmas tree adorned the southwest corner of the room. Clara left to go to the kitchen and George went to climb the small ladder next to the tree and remove the spent candle. Clara returned with a replacement and handed it to George who reached to place it on the tree as he balanced on the ladder.

"I wish New York, Pennsylvania, and a couple of other states wouldn't have rejected Suffrage a couple of weeks ago," said Clara.

"Very disappointing," said George as he stepped off the ladder.

"So very nice of you to bring the ladies out, Mr. Fielding," said Clara.

"Yes," said Anna, "I've wanted to come out to see Rose for some time."

"My pleasure. I have found my Model T to be quite handy. Boy, it's a process to start though with all the preparations and levers to set."

"I would have waited to put the tree up next Sunday on the first day of Advent, but I thought it'd be nice to have it ready before Thanksgiving this week," said Clara.

"It's looking very nice," George said as he returned to his chair.

"You are looking better," he said to Rose.

"Thank you. I'm improving. It's been a while now and I'm still working on getting my strength back. Doc Hall said it'll be a while but it'll happen. I am most grateful to Clara and Fred. Soon I'll be able to help around here."

"Not until you're completely healed," insisted Clara.

"I still can't believe the whole thing," said Anna.

"I know." Rose didn't appear to have more to say about it. She took something from her bag. "I almost forgot," she said. "I have something of yours, Anna. Mr. Markley found it in the car he bought from John."

Anna examined the bracelet. "This is pretty, but it's not mine."

"But the inscription?" said Rose.

Anna looked at it. "He never gave this to me. "And it says 'Anne' with an 'e', but I never go by 'Anne'."

"Then we misread it," said Rose.

"I wonder," said Anna holding the bracelet up to examine it more.

"Did the engraver just make a mistake? An 'e' rather than an 'a'?" said Rose.

"Surprising," said Anna. "This is from Crawford's."

George leaned forward. May I see the bracelet?"

"Of course," said Anna as she handed it to him.

He looked it over for a minute.

"Something, George?" asked Rose.

"No, like Anna said, it's pretty. Interesting that Crawford's would make a mistake like that. They're known for their precise work."

"Well, it doesn't matter," said Rose.

CHAPTER THIRTY

November 25, 1915

Thanksgiving at the Markley Ranch

Two cars pulled up; Clara and Rose watched as women and a couple of men poured out of a Packard and a Ford Model T and headed to the front door.

"Well," said Clara, "I couldn't have gotten everything ready without your help, Rose."

"I enjoyed it and am glad to be helping."

The front door opened to light chatter and laughter. Everyone entered and after exchanging greetings, Clara invited everyone to relax around the living room on the sofa and chairs.

"Kathryn," said Mary, "show everyone what you got."

"Kathryn reached into her bag and pulled out a box camera.

"It's a Brownie," said Margarete.

Kathryn held it up and pointed to the shutter lever, demonstrating how it worked.

"What will you do with it?" said Anna.

"I carry it with me always. I want to take a lot of pictures all around, but with only eight pictures on each roll of film, that would get expensive, so I select wisely. Say, let's use it to get a picture of us all today."

"And we're all dressed up," said Mary.

"This is a special occasion. A good time to get a picture of us."

"Shall we do that in front of the tree and fireplace?" suggested Anna.

"I think we must do it outdoors," said Kathryn. "The pamphlet says it won't work indoors, because it's too dark."

"But it's not dark in here," said Rose.

"The film isn't sensitive enough. You've seen how those photographers use fiery flashes to make enough light."

Rose nodded.

"I will take a picture of all of you with it," said Fred.

They all smiled.

"We have a few minutes until we sit for dinner," said Clara.

The group stood and headed for the front door.

"Where shall we stand?" asked Mary.

Fred pointed to the horizon. "With Sugar Loaf in good view, how about you all stand with it behind you?"

They stood together and Kathryn lined them up to face Fred. After they were ready, Fred said. "Well, let's all look distinguished and smart." He flipped the shutter lever.

"I think that will be nice," he said. "Some of you couldn't resist laughing."

The group burst out laughing more.

"It'll look fine," said Kathryn.

"When does the picture come out?" asked one.

"After I use up all eight pictures on the roll, I take the roll to Dr. Young at Frazier's Pharmacy. He'll get them printed for me. I don't know how long it takes. This is my first roll."

Mary looked over to Sugar Loaf. "Kathryn, you should take your camera when we go up."

"I'm going to try to make it to the top," said Kathryn.

"You will," said George. "I'll keep helping until you reach your goal."

Kathryn muttered a soft, "Thank you."

Clara waited for a moment, then, "Shall we go in for dinner?"

Everyone sat and they said a Thanksgiving prayer. Fred brought a platter in and carved the turkey. After the passing around of dishes and filling plates, Kathryn smiled at George across the table. "I really appreciate all the help with climbing Sugar Loaf, but I want to wait until Rose is well enough to go with us."

"No, Kathryn," said Rose, "you don't wait for me. I'll go soon enough."

"Whenever you ladies are ready to trail up, my hill is your hill," said Fred.

After several mentions of "thank you," everyone started enjoying dinner.

They consumed generous helpings, then relaxed in the living room, some dozing as others engaged in quiet conversation.

Rose got up and sat by Kathryn and Anna.

"Say, Anna," said Rose, "may I ask you a big favor?"

"Anything, Rose."

"If you don't want to go, it's all right, but I left my favorite necklace at my house. It's simple, but precious to me. My grandmother gave it to me on my eighteenth birthday a year before she passed on at such a young age."

"Of course I will," said Anna."

"Anna," said Kathryn, "I'll go get it. I have no connection with that man and it's best if I go."

Anna nodded. "Thank you, Kathryn."

CHAPTER THIRTY-ONE

Early December 1915

Kathryn's Errand

Kathryn inserted the key into the Shanes' front door. It felt wrong to enter someone's house when they weren't there, but she had to do it for Rose. Just a simple favor for a friend. No car parked out front should indicate nobody was home.

She looked around, up and down the street. All quiet as she expected, but it hadn't always been so.

She entered and stepped into someone else's living room. *This is where it happened!* She couldn't avoid imagining the awful scene as it played out in her mind. Then a surge of adrenaline sent her toward the bedroom. Her leg was stiff, but she had learned to live with that and it didn't keep her from being active, marching in Suffrage rallies, trailing up hills—some anyway—hopefully sometime, that all-important one west of town.

On into the bedroom of her friend. Now she really felt uncomfortable. A nightgown sat draped across the far side of the unmade bed. She didn't expect or want to encounter anything like that and she gazed at it for a moment. An expensive one certainly. Enough—on with the task now and get out of here. She went to the vanity and looked at the open jewelry case with necklaces displayed, one gold chain with a rose pendant. The very thing! She lifted it from the case. As she stepped by the bed, she tucked the necklace into her bag. That nightgown on tangled sheets darted into her vision and she glanced at it again.

"That would look nice on you."

Kathryn jumped.

John!

"Oh! Rose sent me over for her pendant," Kathryn said. She tucked it securely down into her bag.

"How kind of you. You are welcome to try on that nightgown. I never told you what a pretty girl you are and you'd look lovely in it. How is that leg of yours?"

Kathryn cringed, then eyed the bedroom door and tucked the bag tightly under her arm. Perhaps she would try a diversion.

"Well now, John, maybe so." She repositioned herself near the door and faced him. "Why don't you get that lovely nightgown and hand it to me and shall I try it on?"

He reached over the bed for it. Kathryn made her move pivoting toward the door, enduring the leg stiffness, trying her best to dash through the living room. He caught up just as she reached the front door and once onto the porch, he pounced and knocked her down.

She managed to sit up and rest on her hands while catching her breath as he stood a few feet away panting, his hair a mess.

A young woman came up the steps and stood next to him.

"Who are you!" she said, staring down at Kathryn. "Oh, John, what happened? She didn't damage anything, did she? Are you all right?" she ran her fingers through his hair.

"I'm fine, Anne, my Sweet."

Kathryn's bag sat on its side. "I hope my things in here are all right," she said as she reached inside to make sure the necklace was in good shape then fumbled with the camera, slid it around and secured it within the other items in the bag. Satisfied, she gathered the bag and sat forward.

"This woman is leaving," John said. "She just came over to get something for Rose and I caught her going through our things."

Kathryn grabbed hold of the porch railing and stood. "John," she said, "is Anne the woman who you're cheating with on the woman that you're cheating with on Rose?" She turned to Anne. "You're the woman I saw next to John at church one time when Rose was nearby."

"Shut up, you pug-ugly girl!" he said.

"I've heard that one," Kathryn said, "and you just tried to cheat on Anne with me?"

Anne gasped.

"She's deranged," he said. "Get on out, Kathryn." He turned to Anne. "I would never do that, my Sweet."

"That's a lovely nightgown on the bed, Anne," Kathryn said. "When John asked me to try it on, I don't think he would have liked my leg." She lifted her hem up just over the knee revealing her impaired leg, Anne gasped again.

John peeked for a moment then turned away. Anne held her hand over her mouth.

"You're right, I don't like it," he said. "Go on, get out."

"Good riddance, you disgusting sap." Then to Anne, "Glad to meet you. I have to get down to my shop."

John sneered at Kathryn. She held her bag tightly and limped across the porch to the steps, hobbled down them to the front walk.

John took Anne's hand. "Come on," he said.

Kathryn looked up at her. "I co-own Main Street Bookshop with Mary Dodd," she said. "Come by sometime."

Anne smiled back while John led her inside.

Kathryn left and went downtown.

Main Street wasn't busy now. She stepped off the curb far enough to get a good view of downtown and took the Brownie out to take a picture. When she got close to the bookshop, she went across the street and took a picture of the shop. That was the last picture on the roll so she took it to the drug store to leave it with Dr. Young for processing.

CHAPTER THIRTY-TWO

January 1916

Women's Club at the Markley Ranch

Everyone gathered around Kathryn when she pulled the pictures out of her bag and held the first one up.

"I wish I'd had my camera when we went to Washington, DC," she said. She set the stack of photos on the coffee table. "Mary, why don't you start passing them around as I hand them to you?"

Mary took a good look at the first photo and passed it to Anna.

"That's looking up Main Street," said Kathryn.

She handed Mary the next photo. "This is another view of Main."

"There's Weber's and you can see Frazier's Pharmacy," said Anna.

"This next one is of the bookshop," said Kathryn. "And now, the one you've all been waiting for. Here we are at Thanksgiving."

A chorus of "Oooo" followed.

Everyone eagerly stood over Anna's shoulder when she held it.

"There we are!" said Margarete.

"I think we look good, even with some of us smiling and some not," said Rose.

They took turns holding the photo and staring at themselves for a couple of minutes.

"Maybe we could have had several taken to have pictures for all of us."

"I have the negatives," said Kathryn. "Dr. Young can make copies from those."

"I'll pay for a copy," said Anna.

Kathryn pulled out the last photo from the stack. "And I have a picture you'll all find interesting." She held up a photo of John and Anne she had secretly taken of them standing before her on the Shane porch.

Rose shrieked. Oh my!"

"I know her," said George when the photo reached him.

"Who is she?" asked Kathryn.

"She was a student of mine. Graduated in 1910. Very bright. Her name is Anne."

"He called her that and added 'my sweet'," said Kathryn. "Now she's John's newest girlfriend."

"How disgusting he called her that," said Anna, echoed by Rose.

"This surprises me about Anne," said George.

"Don't be surprised," said Anna. "It's easy to fall under his spell."

CHAPTER THIRTY-THREE

February 1916

Rose's Move

O n a mid-February day, Kathryn and Rose stood in the Markley living room.

Rose sighed.

"We're going to help you move your things," said Kathryn. "And I can't wait for you to move into my house, so be assured you're welcome."

"I worried about wearing out my welcome with Clara and now your generosity," said Rose.

"Not at all," said Kathryn. "We love you, Rose. I've thought about how nice it'd be to have a housemate for quite some time. Mary and I talked about it, but she's interested in courting someone which could always lead to marriage. But I don't have those aspirations right now."

"What if John tries to prevent me from taking my things and claims he owns what I have?"

"Our grandmothers had to worry about that before the Women's Property Act gave us the right to own our things and make our own money. Don't worry, your heirlooms are safe with their connection to your ancestors, not to mention your jewelry. In fact, you might even be able to take any jewelry meant for his mistresses although you want to check with an attorney on that."

"I don't want those. I prefer my own." Rose twirled the rose pendant between her thumb and finger.

Autumn 1895 – Atchison, Kansas

Ruth Bilson led her granddaughter down the porch steps to the shade of the big oak tree in the middle of the front yard and reached to gently straighten Rose's shoulders.

"Thank you so much for my birthday party, Nana," said Rose.

"Well, we turn eighteen only once, don't we?" She stepped back and reached into a bag. "Now stand up straight, dear, stay still, and close your eyes."

Rose complied and Nana placed a gold chain necklace across Rose's chest, reached around to fasten the clasp behind her neck, then stood back.

"There. It's lovely on you."

Rose took hold of the rose pendant, held it out.

"Nana! It's beautiful!" She thanked her and threw a hug around her."

"Something to remember me by. Whenever you look at it, think about our perseverance. Never give up your goals whatever comes your way."

"I'll treasure it forever," said Rose.

February 1916

"Then it's all set," said Kathryn. "George will help us and Violette said Alan will help, too."

"I'm overwhelmed. It's so nice here, but it'll be good to live in town again."

"I envy your experience to live out here in the hills for a while. George knows a man with a truck and they'll go by your house and load up your things. You might wait until then to go over in case John's home so you'll have George and Alan with you. I'll meet you there, too."

Fred pulled up in the Packard.

"Well," said Rose, "I have to say I'll miss the Markley hospitality, but now I can get back to at least helping take care of a home."

Clara came in from the bedroom Rose was using. "I checked all around and I didn't find anything you're leaving behind, but I'll keep anything I find safe for you."

* * *

Rose looked around at Kathryn's living room and felt the hominess of her new residence.

"Relax on the sofa for a moment first then I'll show you your bedroom," said Kathryn. "Tomorrow, why don't you walk to the bookshop with me. I find that frequent walks are good for my leg. That might be good for you, too."

"That's a wonderful idea. Perhaps we'll take regular walks. Now that John and I are separated, I won't be at his beck and call."

"With definite proof of his affairs in that photo with Anne and the bracelet inscription plus our discoveries on the Promontory, you should have no problem filing the divorce and getting alimony."

Rose lowered her head. "It's so unbelievable," she said. "I never expected this. I tried to be a good wife and make him happy."

"It's going to take a while," said Kathryn. "You've healed physically and your mind needs healing, too. You have good friends in us and we'll help you all we can."

"I'm lucky to call you my friends."

"And we are lucky to call you our friend."

A knock at the door. Kathryn got up to answer.

"Anne! Please come in!"

Kathryn introduced Rose and offered to Anne to sit. "What brings you by, Anne?" said Kathryn.

"John proposed to me." She held up her finger to show an engagement ring. "I haven't given him an answer yet."

"Well," said Rose, "that was my engagement ring. He bought me a new ring on our fifth anniversary and I put my older one in my jewelry case.

"I would never have accepted it if I'd known. I took it just to wear while I thought about his proposal. I know that's not right, but he took my hand and slid it on. I didn't want to jerk my hand back or give any indication until I told him my decision."

"Well?" said Kathryn. "I know I'm being bold, but are you leaning one way or the other?"

Anne took a deep breath. "I'm leaning far away. After what I saw him do to you, Kathryn, I've made my decision. He said he and Rose are separated, so I'll give him this ring back—wait, no, I'll give it to you, Rose."

"I don't know," said Rose. "Maybe."

"We'd better get your jewelry case out of that house but soon," said Kathryn. "Can you stay a while, Anne?"

"Yes. Would you tell me more about the Women's Club?"

CHAPTER THIRTY-FOUR

February 1916

Move Out

"I don't think anybody's home," said Alan Stephens on a mild February day outside the Shane front door. Alan and George unlocked the door and stepped inside.

"It doesn't look like anybody lives here," said George as he looked around the empty living room. "John must have sold the furniture."

"Wouldn't surprise me," said Alan. I know him. He said things on our fishing outings. I always thought he was a decent man, but he said things that made me wonder."

Rose returned from looking around the house. "The dining room table and china cabinet are gone! And Uncle Ralph's desk!"

The front door opened and Kathryn walked in. "Yes, He's selling things all over town—Rose?"

Rose was frantic. "I have to check my jewelry!"

They rushed to the bedroom. The vanity was gone as was the bed and bed stands. The cedar chest sitting by a window was all that was left. Rose opened it. Empty except for her jewelry case. She sighed in relief and reached in to open it.

"About half of the jewelry I kept here is gone. Apparently, John took only the pieces I rarely wore, except there was a ring Aunt Julia gave my mother that is missing. Kathryn, I am so grateful to you for saving my rose pendant and chain."

"I'm so glad," said Kathryn.

They went through the house and found some dishes and Rose's tea set on a counter. The ice box was gone as was the stove.

"He cleared most everything out," said George.

"It's not right," said Kathryn. "Those were Rose's things, too."

"I don't know what I can do about it," said Rose.

"Demand half the proceeds from the sales," said Alan.

"I don't know if it's worth the trouble, although I'll need money to live on until we get a divorce," said Rose.

"I'm not going to charge you room and board," said Kathryn.

"Thank you, Kathryn."

"Say, it's warm for February and I am up for a walk if you'd all like to go to the park," said Kathryn.

A chorus of yeses followed.

"I read this is the warmest February on record according to the National Weather Service," said Rose. "Ice reported broken up in the Kansas River and tributaries.

"Wouldn't it be nice to have this every year?" said George.

"I'll take that jewelry case out to the truck," said Alan. "And George, shall we carry that cedar chest out?"

Kathryn and Rose welcomed the walk to the park. Rose had to stop along the way to rest. She held onto the lamppost at the corner of Second and Main near Weber's Grocery.

"I'm still not fully fit," she said.

Kathryn sensed her disappointment. "Rose, it still takes time. It did with my leg. You just keep at it more every day until it's easier."

"I'm determined to."

They waited with her for a few minutes then everyone headed south toward the park.

When they reached it, Rose pointed toward the far end. "Not there."

"I remember," said Kathryn.

They went to a closer bench in the shade.

Mary walked up to them. "Hi, Everybody!"

They explained to her what happened at Rose's house.

"I'm so sorry, Rose. You know what else? Anne came by the shop. Nobody knows where John is. She thinks he might be in Mound Grove, because he had asked anne to go there with him."

"He's still supposedly waiting on her answer to his proposal."

"I believe it's 'no'," said Kathryn.

CHAPTER THIRTY-FIVE

March 1916

John's Jaunt

Nellie closed the door to the Wichita studio tenement. Clothes and dishes strewn about gave the one-room apartment a funny smell.

She went to the window and looked down at the curb along her street. "Where's your fancy car, John?"

"I parked a ways down."

"Good to have you back," she said as he sat on the bed. "Haven't seen you for quite some time."

"I've been busy."

Well, I'm glad you're back," she said. "Same price as usual, all right?"

John retrieved payment and laid it on her bedside table. The bills flopped in the breeze from the open window.

"How are you doing these days, my dear?" she said.

"I'm fine. A little trouble at home."

"Just relax now and don't worry about it."

* * *

After their session was over, she stood and rubbed his shoulder. "If you want an all-night next time, that costs double."

"I don't know if I will. I'm a little strapped now."

"That's a surprise. The suave and successful John Shane? I even have clients here in Wichita who know of you and your achievements. What happened?"

"Hm. I've run into a snag."

"You'll rebound."

"I should. I might move over here and start anew."

"You'll have competition, but I'm sure you can handle that."

"Say, Nellie, what if we get a place together? I've always liked you."

"That's quite impossible, dear. I have my work."

"I don't mind. We could get a bigger place and I'll keep to my own room and space or go out when you have work."

She picked the money up off the table and found a train ticket stub mixed in. "So am I to carry the rent of that bigger place myself? I do well, but not that well. I can't afford a former investment big shot sponging off me."

"That's not it at all." He noticed her examining the ticket stub. "I took the train over so no one would see me leave. But you think about it, all right?"

She nodded and finished buttoning up.

"Something else I wanted to ask you. . . ."

"Yes, my dear?"

"What are your views on Woman Suffrage? It's spreading like a prairie brush fire."

"I'm all for it."

His expression dampened. "You, too?"

"It's a good thing. But I have to be careful. I can't march in parades, because my clients might notice me, even if not publicly, they could make things bad for me and for Suffrage. Word gets around in secret first and then I'm exposed in public and I'm through, or worse. Some people, men and women both, don't take kindly to suffragists anyway and then it gets out that I'm a suffragist who's in this business. A lot of anti-Suffrage people are calling suffragists prostitutes and 'whores' anyway and my public presence would confirm that for them. I care too much about Suffrage for that to happen. But to your question, I think it's good if I can help choose who runs our government. With the right people in Washington running the country, maybe there'll be more alternatives for someone like me."

"I don't know," John said. "I'm not for it. Say, I need to go. I'm sorry you're feeling that way about that, but do think about my offer."

"John, that's more like a plea than an offer."

"Goodbye then."

CHAPTER THIRTY-SIX

June 1916

The Park and Nellie's

Kathryn, Mary, and friends sat on a blanket under a tree at the park.

"I think if you keep exercising it, you'll get stronger," said Margarete.

"We haven't been up Sugar Loaf in some time," said Kathryn. "I don't even know if I can do it anymore or ever make it to the top, but even if my leg movement isn't great, things are happening in the Suffrage Movement anyway."

Mary agreed.

"It's true," said Rose. "Jeannette Rankin of Montana is running for Congress as is Kansas' own Eva Harding. Imagine two women in the House of Representatives. Can you?"

"I can imagine it, but I'll celebrate after it happens," said Kathryn.

"Say, I just remembered, Violette told me that when she and Alan were in Wichita, they ran into John at a restaurant. I understand he was boasting about drumming up clients and getting to be a big shot there."

"Has anyone seen him around town here?"

I have," said Kathryn. "At least I think so. I'm sure that was him I saw in church last Sunday."

"I didn't go this time, because I wasn't feeling well" said Rose. "Did you talk to him?"

"No!" said Kathryn. "I have nothing to say to him."

"Of course not."

"He's still around stinking up the town."

Rose chuckled. "He's good at that."

"Anyway," said Kathryn, "I'm looking at more ways to help the Movement. I'm saving up travel money for any events out of town that I or we need to attend."

"Something else you need to do, Kathryn," said Mary, "is get back up on Sugar Loaf. It's been too long and you don't want to lose your newfound abilities there."

"Let's go when the weather cools down."

Meanwhile

John Shane noticed two women sitting in a seat a couple of rows behind him. This train car only had a few passengers so he got up and wobbled down the aisle to them and steadied himself on the seat ahead of them.

"Afternoon, ladies," he said awkwardly tipping his hat with the train shaking him.

They were already engaged in conversation and didn't pause for his interruption.

"Well then," he said, "after hearing what you're talking about, I would expect you to be pug-ugly pigs."

They tried to ignore him and continue their conversation.

"I should be honored to ride with you and straighten you out about those stupid Woman Suffrage ideas."

"I should be compelled to straighten out your crooked views," said one of the women.

"Now, now, you wouldn't speak to me like that if— do you know who I am?"

"You're an ignorant sap," said the other woman.

"But I'm not. Perhaps I can find a way into your hearts. I won my soon to be former wife with the right kind of sweet talk that she loved."

"Apparently you went sour and she had to escape."

"She started seeing other men and broke my heart."

"Do us a favor and break our hearts now," said the first woman.

He started to swing in to slide onto their seat.

The woman pushed against him. "You're not welcome here!"

The conductor started to approach. "Leave them alone! Hey, I recognize you—go on, move to another seat!"

John started to scuffle with the women.

The conductor made his way to them. "All right! That's it! Out the door or the window! Coming up on Kechi. You're off the train there! Don't make trouble or I turn you over to the police there."

"Wichita is right after Kechi," John said. He pointed to the seat across the aisle. "I'll sit over there until we reach Wichita."

He moved to the seat and slid next to the window.

"No—we don't tolerate your kind," the conductor said.

As the train slowed he announced to the mostly empty car: "Kechi. This stop, Kechi." He looked at John. "This is your stop. Get up."

"I want to ride the rest of the way as indicated on my ticket that I paid for."

"The only thing you'll pay for is harassing these ladies by spending time in jail! Now get out or the police will give you a ride to Wichita jail!" The conductor made eye contact with a cop on the platform.

John got up and headed for the exit.

"I bet that's the first smart thing you've done today," the conductor said.

"See what Woman Suffrage does?" John mumbled as he reached the steps.

The conductor waved off the cop and escorted the women out by the cop while John headed into the depot.

"Watch him," the conductor said to the cop. "He needs to stay away from those women."

John found an unclaimed taxi and hired it.

* * *

"You need to start behaving on the train," Nellie said.

"You don't want me to start behaving, do you?" John said with a smirk.

She ran her fingers through his hair. "Of course not. Get all you can from me, love, because I'm thinking of retiring."

"Why?" he said returning the hair gesture. You're so desirable." He found a couple of loose strands in his fingers.

She nodded. "See? I'm getting older. It happens to some women, too. I can no longer compete with younger women and *have* been managing to work extra lately so I can save up more to start taking it easy. I hate to say it, but I'm worn out lately from working so much."

He caressed her shoulder. "You're still beautiful."

"Thank you. Let's go." She led him to her bed.

* * *

He fastened up as she finished dressing. "My offer is still open," he said.

"Your plea?"

"It's not a plea, it's a genuine offer. I'm getting work now. You wouldn't have to, so things would be as they should be and you won't have to worry about that silly Woman Suffrage."

"But I will. I'm going to help with Eva Harding's campaign."

"Who's she campaigning for?"

"No, she's the first woman in Kansas to run for national office."

"What? Some National Women's Party thing?"

"U.S. House of Representatives in the First District. In a few months, I'm going to Topeka to help in any way I can."

"I hope to see you before then, but I think your efforts will prove fruitless."

"I'll see you next time, John. I have another client coming by in a while."

"All right." He grumbled as he left and headed down to the streetcar.

CHAPTER THIRTY-SEVEN

July 1916

Where's Nellie?

John arrived at Nellie's this time without incident and knocked on her door. She didn't answer.

After continuing to knock for a minute, he leaned against the door. "Nellie? It's John. I know I didn't let you know ahead of time that I was coming over, but if you're available, I've got some time."

A woman with her hair tied up and her young child emerged from an apartment down the hall.

"She's not home!" she said.

"Do you know when she'll be back?"

"No, I don't. Now, stop making such a racket. I have a young-in finally down for her nap! Go on home. Who knows if she'll be back."

"But—"

"Now, get! Twenty-three skidoo!"

John shrugged and went down the steep wooden stairs to the narrow entrance hall and sat on a dusty step.

"Maybe she's just out for a bit or worse yet she's in Topeka working on that woman's campaign," he mumbled.

He waited for a while, the main door opened, and a woman walked in.

The Road to Sugar Loaf: A Suffragist's Story

"Are you waiting for someone?" she asked.
John looked up the stairs.
"She's not there. She died yesterday."
"What happened? Was it some kind of mishap?"
"I'd say so. She was sick."
"Oh wow—then are you available?"

CHAPTER THIRTY-EIGHT

September 1916

An Approaching Storm

Kathryn, George, Mary, and Rose made it a ways up Sugar Loaf beneath a gray sky past the Promontory. The skies had started out a picturesque blue with puffy clouds that billowed up. Now, dark clouds hurried across above as they lumbered along the upper trail.

"Kathryn, you're doing well," said George.

"I'm doing all right by lifting my leg out as I step," Kathryn said. "Rose, are you? I never tired of the view,"

A strong breeze whipped around them.

"I'm doing fine," said Rose.

"If you'll all wait here for a few minutes," said George, "I want to get a look at that western sky."

He ran around the hillside until he was barely visible.

"George, the consummate scientist, isn't he?" said Mary.

"I think he always has been."

He returned out of breath. "Squall line headed here. We should head down. It might hail and the Promontory trees at least might help a little but they could also be a lightning hazard."

"That ledge on it could provide protection," said Kathryn.

"Let's go," said George.

They went down toward the Promontory as clouds raced overhead. George and Mary helped stabilize Kathryn as they tried to hurry down while Rose managed on her own.

When they reached the Promontory, the squall soared over and they started to shelter beneath the trees. Up above, the clouds roiled.

"You don't see that often," said Kathryn.

George went to the edge of the ledge and started to climb down. "I'll check for snakes."

A moment later, he said, "All clear. Kathryn, I'll give you a hand."

They all scooted to the edge and pitched in to help Kathryn down, then all huddled under the overhang as the rain started pelting the land. Kathryn savored this rare opportunity to watch the growing storm from under there, cozy with her friends as the front rolled over. The rain and hail-enshrouded hills grew fuzzy.

"This really grew into something fierce!" said Kathryn.

"Amazing how those puffy little clouds could turn into this!" said Rose.

"Never underestimate what can grow into a storm," said George.

They huddled and watched the rain as it drenched the land until at last it dwindled and receded.

The sky calmed, started to clear a little, and the low but bright sun cast brilliance over the rolling hills vista. They relaxed and gazed at nature's artwork for a while.

"Oh, look!" said Kathryn, pointing east. "I love how the bright sunlit hills stand out against the dark clouds of the back of the storm."

It's a fitting end," said Rose.

CHAPTER THIRTY-NINE

January 1917

Silent Sentinels

One afternoon in January 1917 at the bookshop, Kathryn re-read the telegram and smiled. She finished going through the inventory list. Everything appeared to be in order for Mary.

Mary emerged from the back room. "Is that it?"

"Yes. It's so exciting. I hope I've got everything ready here for you, starting February. And you are sure you don't mind a temporary move to my house to stay with Rose while I'm gone?"

"Now, Kathryn, I've told you I'll do anything to help support this."

"I am so grateful and I know Rose appreciates it greatly."

"I think it'll be fun and George is around to keep us company sometimes."

"I hope you can find the time to keep private company with him."

"Stop it, Kathryn. You embarrass me, hee hee."

"Rose is really coming along well."

"And so are you. Another trip!"

"I'm not going alone."

"I'm glad of that and we'll miss you."

The little bell jingled and Margarete stepped in.

"I got this from the women's boarding house in washington," Kathryn said holding the telegram up. "It's on Twelfth Street about ten blocks from the White House, which is about a mile on foot she says."

"Ida said she heard others from out of town will be joining the picket as well."

"For the better part of a year like we are?" asked Kathryn.

"I'm not sure," said Margarete. And what about Rose?"

"Mary will stay with her at my house while we're gone."

"That's wonderful."

"And Rose is interested in helping out at the shop," said Mary.

"That's a nice idea so she's not home alone all day."

FEBRUARY 1917

In February 1917, Kathryn and Margarete arrived in Washington, DC. The boarding house was a quaint two-story brick house. A few feet separated it from the taller buildings next to it.

"This is darling," said Margarete.

"It's just right."

They stepped up to the front door and went in. The owner greeted them.

"You must be Kathryn and Margarete, the suffragists?"

"Why, yes," said Kathryn.

"And I am Betty. Come with me."

She led them down a long hall with doors lining either side. The house was much deeper than apparent from the front.

"We have a number of suffragists boarding for several months. They walk to the White House together every morning after breakfast. Some of the picketers are from here in DC, and others from elsewhere have been here since early January. The silent protest began on January tenth.

* * *

The next morning, Kathryn, Margarete, and a couple dozen women headed out to the sidewalk and started along Twelfth Street. One carried a batch of rolled up signs. She positioned herself to walk alongside Kathryn and Margarete.

"I am Claire, our group leader," she said. "I have a sign for each of you when we get there."

Kathryn and Margarete offered their thanks and they continued walking.

"What we do," Claire said, "is protest quietly. Rain or shine, whatever the weather, we keep at it. So far, people have largely ignored us and occasionally the President rides past and nods from his limo, but he's toying with us. He wouldn't even consider hearing Inez Milholland Boissevain memorial resolutions last month and his rebuke was insulting."

Ten blocks later, after crossing a somewhat busy Massachusetts Avenue, they walked along the side of Franklin Square.

"Do we have time to stop for a moment?" asked Kathryn.

"I think we can today," said Claire. The others expressed agreement.

The group turned onto one of the walkways into the park and settled on a bench beneath one of the tall trees.

"Thank you, everyone" said Kathryn. "My leg is improving, but sometimes I need to rest it and stretch a little in this cold weather."

No one asked what had happened to her and they mostly made small talk for a couple of minutes.

"Ready, Kathryn?" said Margarete a minute later as they all prepared to move on.

As Kathryn stood, a young woman and man walked by and stopped.

"Are you the protestors?" the woman asked.

"We are some of them," said Claire.

"I support what you're doing," said the woman.

"So do I," said the man.

The couple went on and the group continued walking to their location outside the White House where the picketers stood along the six-foot wrought iron fence. The picketers wore purple, white and gold sashes and held signs and banners.

Kathryn's leg was doing well, still a little stiff from the cold, her coat, gloves, and hat keeping her comfortable. She sat on the little ledge that ran along the fence. Claire unrolled paper signs and handed one each to Kathryn and Margarete. "I think we can find sashes for you this week."

Kathryn looked at her sign. It read: "MR. PRESIDENT, HOW LONG MUST WE WAIT FOR LIBERTY?"

Claire's sign read: "THE TIME COMES TO CONQUER OR SUBMIT, FOR US THERE CAN BE BUT ONE CHOICE. WE HAVE MADE IT."

Claire started stamping her feet to keep warm.

"Here he comes," she said, pointing to a black limo that slowed as it approached.

President Wilson peered out at the picketers, smiled, and tipped his hat. After motioning to his driver to pull over and stop, he opened his window.

"Good morning, ladies," he said. "I would invite you all into the White House for coffee."

Most of the women grumbled followed by a sharp "No!" by Claire.

Others echoed her.

"No!"

"No, thank you!"

"No!" shouted Kathryn as she, Margarete, and others held up their signs.

"No!" shouted another.

"No!"

"No!"

After the rejections faded, the limo pulled away.

"Well," said Claire, "we've progressed from his usual smiles to an invitation, have we?"

"Invitation—for what?" asked a woman next to her. "Maybe a lecture and an attempt to 'set us straight'. That was no invitation."

"No it wasn't," agreed Claire. "We have to be persistent."

MARCH

On the morning of March 4th, Betty had to squeeze everybody together to get the additional women around the breakfast table.

"I don't usually have to make things so crowded like this or have more than two to a room," she said, "but I must say, hats off to your organizer, Alice Paul for getting such a number of picketers to march today. Mine is a small boarding house, but I wanted to help as much as I could. I just wish you had nicer weather"

"We'll endure it," said Claire.

"Picketing around the White House on a day like today is sure to get noticed," said Kathryn.

"I'm glad there'll be a lot of you," said Betty. "And the timing is good since tomorrow is President Wilson's Inauguration Day."

"I wish he would focus and decide in favor of Suffrage," said one woman. "Just when we think he's in support, he says something different."

"That's why we're here, of course," said Margarete.

Several mumbled "Um hmm" and the conversation ended as everyone noticed the time on the wall clock then Claire asked everyone to convene in the living room.

Everyone found a seat. The rain pattered against the windows and the crackling logs in the fireplace provided a good warm up before today's march.

Claire stood. "I managed to hire a large car that can carry fourteen to take us to the site in a couple of trips since there are quite a few of us. This took some doing with all the picketers today."

That was welcomed news to Kathryn.

Claire continued. "I have banners on poles for our Illinois and Kansas contingents," she said fetching them from a corner.

Margarete leaned toward Kathryn. "Did you know?"

"No."

Claire made her way through the room with two poles careful not to knock against the chandelier and brought the Kansas banner pole to Kathryn and Margarete.

"It's best if Margarete carries the pole," said Kathryn, patting her leg.

After a few minutes, Claire ushered everyone toward the front door. Fortunately, no one was lacking in rain gear of some kind. Kathryn anticipated the day's chill and had wrapped her leg in warm cloth to help avoid getting stiff, something Doc Hall had taught her to do.

After they stepped onto the porch, the large car pulled up.

Kathryn tapped Margarete's shoulder. "Recognize that car? It's a large version of John Shane's car."

"His former car," Margarete said with a laugh.

The driver took Kathryn's elbow, led her to the car, and helped her in. They laid the banner poles lengthwise through the cabin between passengers and the driver helped position them.

More women climbed in and they pulled away to sounds of the tires splashing over wet pavement. Kathryn and Margarete took advantage of the portable heater box on the floor between them and placed their feet next to it.

The driver noticed. "It has hot bricks inside. Works well, doesn't it?"

By the time they arrived outside the White House, the rain was still heavy enough that they had to step over puddles to get to where they waited for instruction for placement in the march. Claire came by and led Kathryn and Margarete into the Kansas location on the street near the Iowa delegation.

The line started to move and Margarete held the pole up as they started walking at a fairly slow pace. Kathryn took hold of the pole as well.

They continued around with the White House to their side behind a thin veil of fog and rain. A few trees did nothing to keep the biting sleet from blowing into their faces. To their left, President Wilson's limo drove alongside, then eased through the picket line, making its way in toward the White House gate.

"He acts like we're not even here," said Kathryn. "Like driving around potholes."

They marched through the freezing rain and Kathryn completed the first lap around the White House with minimal difficulty.

"How are you holding up, Kathryn?" said Margarete.

"I'm doing pretty well," said Kathryn. "I should make it six more times around the 'Walls of Jericho'."

They braved the sleet and wind for six more laps and later, a hired car took them back to the boarding house.

A Week Later

On a sunny but chilly March 11th, back at the White House fence, Kathryn held her banner up as cars passed by on Pennsylvania Avenue. A cold breeze cut into her, stinging her face and her feet were cold. People walked by and mostly ignored them. Occasionally, someone stopped to say 'hello'.

"Look," said Margarete, "the estimate of last week's picketing around the White House in *The Suffragist* says a little over a thousand."

"I think marching in sleet got wide coverage, which I'm sure we would have gotten anyway," said Kathryn. She gathered her coat tightly around her and turned to face the sun to gather whatever bit of warmth it offered. She smiled at more cars as they drove by and got an occasional friendly horn or less friendly blast with a shouted insult.

Margarete looked along the sidewalk at a couple of people walking toward them. The woman carried a coffee pot and cups, the man carried something heavy wrapped in a blanket.

"That's the couple we saw in the park," said Margarete.

When they arrived, the woman set the coffee pot and cups on the small ledge behind. The man laid the bundle down and opened it, revealing hot bricks. He placed them on the sidewalk.

"Stand on these," he said to Kathryn. They'll help keep you warm." He poured some coffee, his companion did the same, and they handed the cups to Kathryn and Margarete.

He picked up the blanket and handed it to Kathryn and Margarete. "It's still warm. Wrap it around the both of you."

Several more people came by and extended similar offerings to other picketers.

Kathryn relished the warmth radiating up from the bricks and the coffee was just what she needed.

"I am Genevieve and this is Roscoe," said the woman. "We were happy to hear how well the picket went last week," she said. "We would have been here if we could have. I wish we could stay longer now, but we're going to fetch more hot bricks and coffee for others," she said as they turned to leave.

A car went by and someone shouted, "Go home, woman where you belong!"

The car veered toward the curb, hit a small puddle, and sent a misty spray onto the picketers, their signs and banners.

Kathryn didn't appreciate the familiar gesture. She retrieved a handkerchief and wiped off her face and sign.

APRIL

On April 4th, when they returned to the boarding house for the evening, Betty handed a telegram to Kathryn. She eagerly pulled off her hat, hung it on the coat rack, and started reading.

Margarete tried not to look over her shoulder. "From Mary?"

"Yes," Kathryn said with a smile. "She sent this just after the War Declaration on Germany today. George won't be drafted because he's a teacher."

"Wonderful. He might not have been anyway with his bad leg."

They hung up their coats and headed to the dining room where the conversation focused on the war declaration.

"People are divided on it," said Claire.

"I'm glad Congress approved it," said one.

"I'm not sure what to think," said Margarete.

"Germany sank all those ships, killing a lot of civilians."

"We're supposed to be defending democracy," said Kathryn, "but we don't have democracy in our own country."

"True," said Claire. "I'm worried the war news is overshadowing the Women's Suffrage Amendment reintroduced in Senate a couple of days ago by Congresswoman Rankin of Montana. We must keep up the pressure on the President and Congress."

* * *

On April 20th, President Wilson's car drove by Kathryn and her companions on the picket line.

"He's completely ignoring us now," said Kathryn. Then she pointed to some commotion with several men and picketers down the picket line. Several women cried out.

"What is happening there?" Margarete said.

Claire stepped out to get a view. "Oh my! They're shoving our picketers around!" She stood on tiptoes. "Oh dear! They're hitting some of the women!"

Kathryn turned to stretch her leg on the ledge and started to lay her sign against the fence. A car pulled up and a man jumped out.

He ran up to her and yelled: "Put that sign away! Don't you care—you unpatriotic pug!"

She held onto the sign, he pushed her down, ripped the sign from her hands and tore it up.

"Go home, woman!" he blasted, then pushed her again as she tried to get up and he ran away before Kathryn's companions could nab him.

JUNE

June 20th on the picket line, Kathryn, Margarete, Claire, and several others went to watch Lucy Burns and Dora Lewis who stood by the White House gate holding a very large banner that read: "President Wilson and American envoy Elihu Root are deceiving Russia. The women of America tell you that America is not a democracy. Twenty million women are denied the right to vote…. Tell our government that it must liberate its people before it can claim free Russia as an ally." A large crowd had gathered around the women before the Russian delegation reached the gate.

The crowd turned into an angry mob as the delegation went through the gate. The crowd surrounded the picketers, tore the banner down and ripped it to shreds.

"Look what they're doing!" said Claire.

"They're attacking the women and the police are doing nothing!" said Kathryn.

"I wish we could help," said Margarete.

"We can" said Kathryn. She hurried over to the women. "Please help them!" she shouted to the police.

One of the police officers shrugged. "They'll be all right," he said.

"Once they give this up, they'll be safe at home," another said.

"They're being assaulted!" shouted Kathryn, but the police did nothing. After holding herself back from shoving or hitting one of them, she left and rejoined Margarete.

* * *

Two days later on June 22nd, it was worse. After the Russian delegation fiasco, Kathryn and her companions kept watch on the White House gates. Lucy Burns and Katherine Morey, were demonstrating and drawing a small crowd. A police wagon pulled up, and a policeman got out and went to them.

"They're getting arrested!" shouted Kathryn as the police led the women into the wagon.

"The police ignore us when we're assaulted," said Claire, "now we get arrested for exercising our right to protest?"

Two more cops approached Kathryn and her companions.

"Go home, ladies," he said.

"Why were those two women arrested?" asked Kathryn.

"Obstructing traffic, which is why you'll be if you continue with this." He pointed and frowned at the banners. "What do you think you can accomplish? You've got many people against you, some of them strongly opposed, a lot of them embarrassed by you."

"Embarrassed that half the adults in our county are denied the right to vote," said Kathryn.

"I could tell you a dozen reasons why you don't need or should desire the vote, but I'm sure you've heard them many times."

"Tell me, sir," said Kathryn, "what's your name?"

"Al. My name is Al."

"Well, Officer Al, do you have a wife? Is your mother living? Do you have a sister?"

"I know what you're asking. The women in my life are as divided as the country, but you need to head on out of here." He stepped away and went back to his partners by the gate.

"Well," said Kathryn, "he was polite," she said to Margarete and Claire.

"He's the exception, I'm sure," said Margarete. "We need to be careful."

* * *

On June 24th, Kathryn and her picketing companions managed to avoid arrest, but a police wagon drove by on Pennsylvania Avenue and stopped not far from the White House gate and engaged some picketers. They led one woman after another to the wagon which then drove away. Another drove by and stopped before the gate this time and started to arrest more women.

"They've taken at least a dozen away!" shouted Kathryn unable to contain her anger.

She couldn't run after the police wagon and scream at them—her leg wouldn't allow that, but she laid her banner down and managed a lopsided trot toward the police wagon.

Claire and Margarete yelled after her to stop.

"Let them go!" Kathryn shouted. "We're having a peaceful protest!"

As the policeman closed the door to the wagon, Kathryn reached them. She heard the women crying out from inside to be let out.

Officer Al from the other day grabbed her. "I recognize you. Let's go." He opened the doors and shoved Kathryn into the hot wagon amid gasps and shrieks from the struggling women inside.

"I misjudged you, Al!" she said as she tumbled on top of several women in the stifling dark as the doors closed behind her.

During the dark bumpy ride, crowded with others, she tried to ease her leg into a comfortable position and relief came when the doors opened to bright sunshine in front of a District building. The police led the women into the building, into a room, past desks occupied by uniformed male and female officers, into another room that already had a dozen women standing there, and a man entered and faced them all.

"You've been brought here for obstructing traffic. No charges will be brought against you. You're free to go."

Officer Al and the other cop stood aside and ushered all but several of them out, through the desk room to the tall outer doors of the building. He opened them and waved the women out. Kathryn started to make her way toward the wide steps leading down to the front sidewalk.

As the policemen started to head back inside, one of the women pointed at Kathyn and shouted: "What about giving her a ride back!"

"We're obligated to bring you in," Al said, "not take you back. Go on, you're free to go."

"She's crippled!"

Kathryn hated that word, her main challenge, the one leg.

Al stepped over to her. "All right. We're headed there now, come along."

"I don't want to be a part of what you're doing by riding with you to arrest more women!' said Kathryn.

"We'll let you out at your spot," he said.

"Go!" shouted several women.

She rode squeezed on the seat next to Al and another cop as Al drove.

"What happened to you?" the other cop asked.

"I got arrested for holding a sign," said Kathryn.

"No, I mean your limp."

"Climbing accident."

"Well, you're making things hard for yourself," he said.

"I think I told her that a couple of days ago," Al said. "She didn't listen."

"Mark my words, boys, we will prevail," warned Kathryn.

They chuckled and didn't say more.

Just after they reached the picket line, Al said, "How close do you want us to stop?"

"Here. I'll walk to my spot."

"Suit yourself."

They pulled over and amid shouts from picketers. Al got out and ran around to the passenger door. The other got out and held the door open then Al offered his hand to help her down.

"No thank you," she said. "Where was that courtesy earlier, Al?" She stepped out and the wagon drove away. Picketers swarmed around her asking what happened and was she all right."

"We were arrested for obstructing traffic and not charged," Kathryn said.

She made her way back to her companions to the same questions.

"The worst part was the ride there," said Kathryn. "They had no consideration for us riding in that stifling wagon."

"Lucy Burns and Katherine Morey were released immediately after they were arrested the other day, too," said Claire, "and they were arrested again a few hours ago and released. And look, there they are again, picketing at the gate!"

* * *

On the picket line the next day, Claire had disappointing news. "Six picketers have been sentenced to three days in District jail!"

"Now they're arresting and sentencing us just for exercising our right to protest," said Kathryn. "Look—what's going on there!" She pointed toward the White House gate.

"A policewoman took the banner from that picketer in the white hat," said Margarete. "Now she's trying to take the banner from the woman next to her, but she's not giving it up."

"She's arresting them!" said Kathryn.

"Those picketers are Florence Youmans and Annie Arnie!" said Claire.

JULY

On July 4th, Kathryn, Margarete, Claire, and two other picketers reached the area of the White House gate.

"Phew it's hot," said Kathryn as she stopped and stretched her leg.

"There she is," said Claire.

They went up to a picketer who was holding her banner up high.

"Iris?" said Claire.

"Yes?"

"I am Claire and here are Kathryn and Margarete from Kansas." Claire turned to them. "Kathryn and Margarete, this is Iris Calderhead of Marysville, Kansas."

Kathryn extended her hand. "Of course! I know of you and your work with the NWP and your extensive travel. I'm honored."

"As am I," said Margarete also extending her hand.

Iris took their hands. "So nice to meet you both," she said. "Yes, Suffrage is so important, I travel to convince others of this."

"Thank you, Iris," said Claire as she turned to head back to their spot. Kathryn and Margarete followed her. As they walked, they heard commotion behind them.

Margarete turned around. "They're arresting Iris!"

"This is getting ridiculous!" said Kathryn.

"They'll hopefully give her a short sentence like they've started doing," said Margarete.

"They're imprisoning law-abiding citizens and ignoring those who are committing violence," said Kathryn.

They continued toward their spot. A familiar car went by and someone yelled, "Go home, back to your kitchen!"

"Well, I've been waiting for him," said Kathryn. "He hasn't been by for days."

"I just smile at him," said Margarete.

"Fortunately, he's harmless," said Claire.

"Unlike some," said Kathryn. Then she noticed a policeman approaching a picketer down the other direction.

"Not another one," said Kathryn. She started to walk to there.

"Kathryn, please, no," said Claire.

Kathryn ignored her and reached the picketer who tried to hold onto her banner as the cop was trying to take it from her. Kathryn stepped up to them. In a fairly quiet, worried voice, she mumbled, "If you're arresting this woman because of this banner, I better go tell Mabel to put hers away, with its obscenities."

Kathryn turned to leave and walked along the picket line. The cop followed her and she pretended she didn't know he was there. A minute later, she stopped at an empty spot.

"Where's Mabel?" Kathryn mumbled just loud enough for the cop to hear.

"You lied," he said. "I should take you in."

"I didn't lie about anything," said Kathryn. "I was worried about my friend and came over here to tell her to put that banner away."

The cop grumbled and started walking back to where he was about to make an arrest before.

Kathryn followed and when he didn't find the woman to be arrested, one of the woman's companions stopped Kathryn. "Thank you for what you did," she said, pointing down the picket line. "She hid behind the line until he left, then she stepped out to hold her sign up."

"I'm pleased," said Kathryn. "She'll do more good here than in jail."

Margarete and Claire looked relieved when Kathryn returned.

"Are you all right?" both asked.

"I am fine. There'll be one less arrest today."

AUGUST

August started out a bit cooler than July for a couple of days, but the typical August heat came rushing back and the short cool break didn't help cool rising tensions. By mid-August, things got worse, especially after a new banner rolled out, carried by many picketers for they wanted to be sure the President saw it:

KAISER WILSON

HAVE YOU FORGOTTEN HOW YOU SYMPATHIZED
WITH THE POOR GERMANS BECAUSE
THEY WERE NOT SELF-GOVERNED?
20,000,000 AMRICAN WOMEN
ARE NOT SELF-GOVERNED
TAKE THE BEAM OUT OF YOUR OWN EYE.

On August 14th, Claire held her banner high. "Let's make sure President Wilson sees this new banner." Kathryn and Margarete did the same and when President Wilson's limo passed them, he didn't pay attention. Kathryn leaned out from the sidewalk and held her banner at an angle. She caught a glimpse of him looking at it.

The limo went on toward the gate. She noticed him glancing at the banners as his limo rolled along.

A crowd on foot came down the street. Men jeered and shouted. "If you think you can get away with this, you're fools!"

"You're safe in your homes! Go there and you'll have nothing to fear!"

Kathryn and the others ignored the shouts. In fact, Kathryn found them empowering. She held her banner up.

More cars passed by.

As she turned to speak to Margarete, something smashed into her cheek. Liquid ran down her face. She brought her hand up to the stinging cheek bone. Margarete reached over to her.

"An egg! Are you all right?"

Kathryn pointed to a car pulling away. "It came from that car. Now they're also throwing tomatoes at picketers."

Another car passed by and pulled over ahead. Three men hopped out and rushed the group of women there. One man grabbed a picketer and threw her onto the sidewalk while another slapped and hit her.

Kathryn wiped the egg off and turned toward the violence.

"Kathryn, stay here, don't go to those men."

"I don't have to," Kathryn said, "they're coming here!" She stepped back toward the fence and the wall.

Within moments, the men were pouncing on them. "Where are you going?" one said to Kathryn.

Two of them grabbed Kathryn's shoulders and slammed her against the fence. Margarete, Claire, and another picketer started kicking them and the two men stumbled back. More seemed to come from nowhere and joined in amid shouts of "traitor" and vulgar insults. Now an angry mob surrounded them, pushing Kathryn and her companions to the ground, ripping up banners, kicking the women as they tried to get up.

Kathryn felt a dash of hope as a police wagon pulled up and cops jumped out. They ushered the men away. The mob rushed to the next group of picketers, the police followed, joined the mob, and took part in attacking the women, pulling several picketers into the wagon.

Kathryn felt the whole world crashing down as she and her neighbors lay on ruined banners, some coughing and panting as they caught their breath.

* * *

The next day was only marginally better. After a long day, as Kathryn, Margarete, and Claire started to walk to the boarding house, Claire said, "Let's stop by New Ebbitt Café on the way and have supper there. It's about a block from here."

They reached the restaurant and entered. About half of the occupied tables lined the windows and two rows of tables in the middle stretched to the back beneath wooden ceiling cross beams that were supported by wooden columns.

"How nice," said Margarete, "with white tablecloths."

"It's a favorite spot for politicians and others who come to influence them," said Claire. She spotted a table. "Let's take that one."

They settled onto wooden cane chairs at a table next to one of the wooden columns.

Claire leaned toward the others and discreetly gestured toward a man and a woman sitting next to a window. "Look over there," she said. "That's Congresswoman Jeannette Rankin of Montana and Kansas Congressman Philip Campbell. What must they be talking about?"

"I can imagine," said Kathryn. She scooted her chair back and stood.

"What are you doing?" whispered Claire.

"Introducing myself."

"She's been doing this a lot lately," Margarete whispered to Claire.

Kathryn limped over to the their table. Both looked up, Campbell stood.

"Pardon me," Kathryn said. "I am Kathryn Wolfe from Kansas and I've wanted to meet both of you for some time."

Campbell smiled and offered his hand. "Pleased to meet you. What brings you to Washington?"

"I've been a Silent Sentinel since February."

"Oh!" said Rankin who slid her chair out and stood, offering her hand. "I applaud your bravery."

"As do I, Miss Wolfe," said Campbell. "Be assured we are working to influence our colleagues to favor Suffrage."

"I am optimistic," said Rankin.

"If you are, and you, Mr. Campbell, then so am I," said Kathryn. She bowed and went back to her table.

"She said she applauds our bravery," said Kathryn when she returned.

"Glad to know," said Claire. "And I applaud your bravery in approaching them."

"Well, look," Kathryn said, looking over at Rankin and Campbell who approached.

"Don't get up," said Rankin. "We just wanted to meet your friends, Miss Wolfe." She looked at Kathryn's companions. "Are you all from Kansas?"

Claire gestured to the rest at the table. "They are. I'm from Maryland."

"Oh?" said Campbell. "One of the satellite cities just outside the District?"

"Actually, I'm from the town of Williamsport."

"I know of it," said Campbell. "There's a John Brown connection there. So there's a historical link between Williamsport and Lawrence, Kansas, and Harper's Ferry."

Rankin tapped Campbell's elbow and they excused themselves to leave.

When Kathryn and her companions finished their meal, the sun was still up.

* * *

Back at the boarding house, Betty gave Kathryn a telegram. Kathryn was tired after the hard day so she took the telegram to the living room, settled onto a comfortable chair and opened the correspondence.

Claire entered the room. "May I join you?"

Of course." Kathryn gestured to the chair next to her.

"I got word that the women who were arrested yesterday received sixty-day sentences and two men were arrested."

"Oh dear, sixty days. What will be our strategy?"

"Maybe Alice Paul has one. . .well, I'll leave you to your letter."

"No, Claire, please stay."

Kathryn silently read the telegram.

SYCAMORE FALLS KAN AUGUST 15 1917

KATHRYN WOLFE
BETTY'S 12TH STREET BOARDING HOUSE WASHINGTON DC

SADDENED TO LEARN OF TERRIBLE ATTACK. GLAD YOU'RE ALL RIGHT.

WE MISS YOU AND MARGARETE. UNDERSTAND YOUR MOTIVATION TO STAY LONGER. PLEASE BE CAREFUL.

ALL IS WELL HERE. BOOKSHOP STAYING BUSY. YOUR HOME IS COMFORTABLE. ROSE IS WELL.

JOHN SHANE CAME BY SHOP. DIDN'T CAUSE TROUBLE. WANTS ROSE BACK. SHE WON'T HAVE HIM.

BE WELL
- MARY

SEPTEMBER

September was a continuation of August as the attacks from mobs and arrests of picketers continued. Kathryn and her companions avoided arrest and received a few distressing injuries from attackers. The police didn't help and continued to join in on the attacks and harassment.

On Sunday evening, September 30th, the women gathered in discussion in the living room at the boarding house.

"How is your leg doing, Kathryn?" asked Claire.

Kathryn patted her leg. "It's better. It's been about a week and a half now since the mobs last attacked and the police joined in."

"It was horrible," said Caire.

"I was very vocal in the picket line and I shouted things I never thought I'd say at the crowds who cheered on the arrest. That was the day Genevieve joined us."

"I remember it well," Genevieve said. "I was new and wanted to join in on the shouting, but wanted to get accustomed to the picketing before I did that. I was scared when the mob attacked us."

"It's all right. You avoided getting hurt that day by being careful, Genevieve," said Kathryn. "I was so enraged at the arrest, I couldn't stop yelling insults at the police. One cop pounced on me during the mayhem and stomped on my right leg. You know what the sap said? 'I saw your limp. How about the other leg to even things out, pretty girl?' I was lucky he didn't break it, but that awful bruise is just now starting to fade."

"And yet," said Claire, "after an awful month, just four days after Alice's arrest, the House of Representatives created a separate Woman Suffrage Committee to allow suffragists to bypass the House Judiciary Committee. Now the Judiciary Committee won't be able to postpone Suffrage bills like they've done to prevent the bills being brought to the floor. And since the Senate already had its Woman Suffrage Committee, now that the House also has theirs, so much the better for our chances."

"Senator Joseph Walsh opposed its creation," said Kathryn, "saying the House was yielding to the nagging of iron-jawed angels and referred to Silent Sentinels as bewildered, deluded creatures with short skirts and short hair."

The room erupted in laughter.

Then Claire said, "Senator Andrieus Aristieus Jones went to the Occoquan Workhouse a couple of weeks before to check on reports of Suffrage prisoners being mistreated and then the next day the committee suddenly reported the Suffrage bill was on hold for six months."

After they chatted for a while, Kathryn yawned. "I believe I'll turn in," she said.

"You mean," said Claire, "we don't get to hear about that little mountain of yours tonight? Sugar Loaf?"

"It's not a mountain, but a hill" said Margarete.

"True," started Kathryn. "George says latest survey data shows an eight to nine hundred foot rise from nearby land to the top of Sugar Loaf."

"That's interesting, Margarete," said Claire. "The elevation change from my town in Maryland to the summit of Fairview Mountain in the Alleghenies isn't a lot more than that."

Kathryn sighed and went to bed.

OCTOBER

Autumn cool prevailed as October wore on, but arrests continued at their usual pace along with mob attacks. Kathryn and her companions were growing fatigued from that and had to summon their inner strength to continue picketing. After all, they were making some progress, although triumphs were often answered by defeats or tragedies.

One October day, Kathryn, Margarete, and Claire occupied their usual place a ways from the White House gate.

Kathryn held her banner up, starting the day to an occasional car splashing followed by shouts from the offending car. She could handle that and just kept at it, holding her banner high, sometimes smiling. And then her mood crashed.

Officer Al approached from a ways down. She wasn't sure whether to duck back or move from her spot and try to avoid him, but decided to face him anyway as he walked up to her.

"Hello, Kathryn," he said. "I hope you are well."

His demeanor surprised her. "Hello, Officer Al, dare I ask what brings you here today?"

He reached into his jacket and produced a folded piece of paper.

"I am in contact with one of the prison guards at Occoquan Workhouse," he said quietly, holding the paper between folded arms while pretending to be being enraged. "The women still aren't being treated well. They started a secret petition and that guard I'm in contact with, one of good character, got word to me to visit the workhouse and smuggle this out. The Suffragettes in there are demanding political prisoner status. I can't do anything with this paper, so I'll give it to you, so that you or somebody can present it to the District Commissioners." He folded it tightly with one hand and reached to Kathryn and pretended to grab her hand.

She forced a scowl as she clinched the paper and brought her hands together as if to rub them. "Thank you, Al," she said, "it appears I didn't misjudge you after all."

"Well," he with a wink, "if you keep this up, you'll see me again!"

His partner came to them. "Run 'em in, Al?" the partner said, frowning at Kathryn as he started to reach toward her.

"No, we've got more militant ones to nab."

"Yeah, let's go."

Claire came over to Kathryn. "I thought he was going to take you away," she said, "with what he said about seeing you again."

Kathryn stepped back against the little wall and sat with Claire.

"Are you all right?" asked Claire.

"I am quite well, thank you. "I think he means he might see me again to help the cause." She slipped the folded paper to Claire.

NOVEMBER

In the November 6th chill, Kathryn started to hold her banner up. A group of men walked by along the street. As they approached Kathryn and her companions, Officer Al trotted over to her.

"I'll keep those men away by being here for now," he said.

Kathryn stepped back so she was shielded from view of the men by her companions.

"Something, Al?" she said.

He spoke softly. "Alice Paul and Rose Winslow started a hunger strike yesterday to protest the rejection of their demands to be treated as political prisoners. The women are being housed in horrible conditions. Word is getting out about it." He raised his voice and stepped back. "I meant what I said!"

* * *

By November 10th, the treatment of the jailed suffragists was in the news and Kathryn could feel the tension among the picketers.

As the morning progressed, she and her companions moved closer to the White House gate and congregated with other groups to form a large protest while other groups went to the Capitol building.

The large group of picketers around Kathryn held banners that said: **WE DEMAND THAT THE AMERICAN GOVERNMENT GIVE ALICE PAUL A POLITICAL OFFENDER, THE PRIVILEGES RUSSIA GAVE MYUKOFF.**

Police swarmed around them with several wagons parked there. Kathryn watched for Officer Al, but he wasn't visible among the developing chaos.

A cop arrested one picketer, then another cop arrested an older picketer.

Another cop came up to Kathryn. "Surrender your sign," he said.

"I won't," she said, pointing to a distant group. "You should see those vulgar signs over there."

"I've heard about your deceptions," he said. "No deal, you're coming with us. Drop the banner and get in the wagon."

This wagon had windows with bars unlike the one that took her away in summer.

A police guard led Kathryn and other fellow suffragists into Judge Alexander Mullowney's courtroom for fast sentencing.

* * *

Everyone stood when Judge Mullowney entered and took his seat on the bench.

Lucy Burns faced him.

"Lucy Burns, the court sentences you to thirty days in prison for each of three criminal offenses of obstructing traffic to be served consecutively."

Burns held her head up while a guard led her away in handcuffs.

The sentencing continued. Dora Lewis and Eunice Dana Brannan each received sixty-day sentences.

Mary Nolan who was the oldest there, faced Judge Mullowney.

He pulled on his pointed goatee and adjusted his glasses. "Mary Nolan, for the crime of blocking traffic, the court sentences you to pay a fine of twenty-five dollars or spend six days in prison. Given your age, I urge you to pay the fine and avoid prison."

She stood on her tiptoes in a dignified stance. "Your Honor, "I have a nephew fighting for democracy in France. He is offering his life for his country. I should be ashamed if I did not join these brave women in their fight for democracy in America. I should be proud of the honor to die in prison for the liberty of American women."

Judge Mullowney was moved and appeared to hold back emotion at her statement resting his head in his hands while the guard led her away.

All but some of the remaining received thirty-day sentences. Three received fifteen day sentences.

Kathryn faced Judge Mullowney.

"Kathryn Wolfe, for the crime of obstructing traffic, the court sentences you to thirty days in prison or pay a fine of twenty-five dollars."

"I decline to pay the fine," she said, holding her head up. Kathryn's fellow suffragists were inspiring to her. Lucy Burns and particularly Mary Nolan, who would despite her age choose prison for the cause rather than take the easy option of paying the fine. Kathryn limped along as the guard led her out to wait however long it would take to be transferred to prison.

CHAPTER FORTY

November 1917

The Night of Terror

On November 15th, in the dying twilight of evening, Kathryn could barely make out the forbidding squat structures of Occoquan Workhouse where she and about thirty of her fellow suffragists were headed for conviction of the false crime of obstructing traffic. When they reached the building, the overgrown bushes and weeds along a porch greeted them. Kathryn could barely see them in the dark.

The guards took them all across the porch into an office to be processed. Mrs. Herndon stood behind a desk with several men present in the room. Many of the women were so tired they sat or lay on the floor.

Dora Lewis often spoke for the group.

"If you please, I must speak to Mr. Whittaker," she said to Mrs. Herndon.

"You'll sit here all night then," Mrs. Herndon said.

Men started gathering on the porch outside the door.

"Mary Nolan," Mrs. Herndon called to the women.

Mary didn't answer her.

The door burst open. Superintendent Whittaker and a number of men in ragged clothes entered, one after another.

Dora stood. "If you please—"

"You shut up," Whittaker said. "I have men here to handle you." He shouted at the men, "Seize her!"

His men pounced on Dora and dragged her out the door.

"They have taken Mrs. Lewis!" someone yelled.

One man lunged at Mary Nolan and grabbed her shoulder.

"I'll come with you, don't drag me, I have a lame foot," she said.

Several men jerked Mary out the door, down the porch steps into the dark of night.

Several more men dragged other women out.

Two men came to Kathryn.

"Please," she said, "My leg is impaired. I'll go willingly."

"I've heard that before," said one. The men dragged her out, down the steps, through the dark to another building. It was lit up now and the American flag flying above was visible in the light from a window. They dragged her so fast into the building to a large room that she had to keep positioning her leg just right to protect it. From the large room, she could see into a wide hallway lined with stone cells.

They dragged her, Mary Nolan, and others past two men holding frail Dorothy Day. They twisted Dorothy's arms above her head and slammed her over the arm of an iron bench. Twice.

Dorothy then lay there with her arms out catching her breath.

"The damn Suffrager!" yelled one man. "My mother ain't no Suffrager! I'll put you through hell!"

A uniformed man with a heavy stick growled from the hall, "Damn you, get in here."

Several men dragged Kathryn and others over to the wide hallway.

Kathryn struggled to maintain a comfortable leg position as they pulled her along toward the end of the hallway. There they hoisted Mary Nolan onto her feet and threw her into a cell. She lost her balance and fell against the iron bed. They dragged Kathryn to the cell across from Mary's cell and threw her into the dark, filthy cell. She tumbled to the dirty cement floor and managed to sit up on a metal bed. The guards threw in a mat and a dirty blanket.

They brought Alice Cosu and shoved her into the same cell with Mary Nolan where Alice hit the wall.

They cared nothing about her condition and threw Dora Lewis in like a large sack of flour causing her head to hit the iron bed frame, knocking her out.

"She's dead!" Mary Nolan screamed.

"Dora's not moving!" shouted Alice.

Kathryn almost hyperventilated watching the brutality.

Moments later, Dora stirred.

Alice doubled over, clutched her chest, gasped, and collapsed.

"Please!" Mary screamed. "We need a doctor!"

"Please help!" shouted Kathryn, but the guards ignored them.

Cries echoed throughout.

An administrator came by and looked in. Dora and Mary asked for a doctor again.

"No," he said.

He turned to Kathryn.

"Please get Alice help right away. We think she had a heart attack," Kathryn said.

"Other prisoners aren't your concern."

When he left, she set the mat on the metal bed, sat and stretched her leg. As she rubbed it, she heard clanking sounds down the hall followed by the slamming of people against cell bars and shrieks. The commotion drew closer with a male voice and a woman's pleading that went unanswered, then she cried out.

Mary and Dora kept calling out, begging for a doctor for Alice who was vomiting now.

Footsteps drew closer.

He stopped at Mary, Dora, and Alice's cell. "No doctor," he said.

Turning to Kathryn, he unlocked her cell door, which lifted her spirits until he entered the cell. "Stand up," he said. "Step over to the bars."

Kathryn complied.

"Reach up." He pulled out a pair of handcuffs.

"What are those for?"

"Shut up and put your wrists together."

He handcuffed her wrists to the bar above her head.

"My leg is tired and hurt," she said with a groan.

"You'll get used to it."

"What!"

"Just relax and have a good stretch."

"But my leg is impaired and I can't stand on it for a long time!"

"Seems strong enough for your all-day protests. This'll teach you to stop that nonsense. And no talking to the other prisoners or you'll be gagged and placed in a strait-jacket. Your leader knows this, too, and she'll be sleeping like this."

"I won't talk to anyone. Please un-cuff me."

He kicked her leg, stood there, and snickered.

"Nighty night."

More commotion down the hall grew louder with screams.

"Good," he said as another guard with a club showed up outside her cell and came in.

"Give me that club," the first guard said. He smashed the club against Kathryn's shoulder. The other guard took the club and hit her other arm. Then they left and made their way along the corridor where they met others. They entered a neighboring cell and started beating the women there. They went back up the hall and beat more prisoners.

Cries and moans echoed through the corridors into the night. Kathryn felt nauseous.

She was very worried about Alice.

Chilly air wafted down the hallway which made it hard to endure being chained while standing, wrists bound above. She switched to her right foot to relieve her left and alternated between legs as the night wore on.

It seemed forever as she shifted on her feet during the long night. She entered lulls of consciousness, sometimes almost passing out but secured upright by the handcuffs, waking when her body started to collapse. After a long wait, the perpetual night yielded to the soft glow of morning light that gradually emerged in the hallway.

A different guard came by and entered Kathryn's cell. She shivered and felt sick, her leg and shoulder hurt.

"Someone will be by with breakfast," he said, then removed the handcuffs. She barely made it over to use the toilet. It had to be flushed from outside the cell. She shifted to the bed exhausted. She wanted her toothbrush and a comb for when she felt better.

A few minutes later, someone brought some toast and a plate of fruit. The fruit was full of maggots. The sight of it made her want to vomit. She set the plate aside and leaned forward to see who was coming down the hall now.

A doctor arrived to examine Alice. Finally.

* * *

When evening arrived, Kathryn thought she heard whispering. She put her ear between the bars toward the hallway. Whispers cascaded from cell to cell. Someone in the cell next to hers whispered over to her. "We're going on a hunger strike until they treat us better and grant political prisoner status."

Kathryn whispered the message to the next cell.

They stopped whispering when a guard showed up nearby. He brought a plate to Kathryn and like the previous plate, the food had maggots and insects crawling through it. Still feeling bad from the night, the sight of it made her sick.

"No," she said. "Take it away."

November 25th

After more than a week of fasting in appalling conditions, Kathryn woke early, dozing for a few minutes and watched through droopy eyes the shaft of sunlight crawling along the hallway outside her cell. Today started the twelfth day of her hunger strike and she managed to be one of the hunger strikers who weren't force fed like at the District jail. In any case, she had never done this before and she drank water not knowing if that was "allowed" in such a strike. She could feel the toll that fasting was taking on her. Her muscles were losing strength and it was hard getting up to use the toilet. She drifted back to sleep, awakened when a guard came into her cell with a plate of food. "No," she said with a raspy voice.

She appreciated the demeanor of this guard. "You're among the group prisoners being released today," he said. "The rest will be released tomorrow. Have a bite, but that's all until a prison doctor examines you."

She hadn't fasted as long as some of the other prisoners and probably could sit up. She did and felt a little dizzy. The guard gave her some water and kneeled next to her. "Alice Paul is being released from the District jail today as well along with other Suffragettes. She's been fasting since October and she's not doing well."

"Why some tomorrow?" asked Kathryn. "Why can't everyone be released today? I don't feel right going before my sisters. And by the way, the word 'suffragist' is preferred. Not 'Suffragette'."

"My apologies."

"Are you the—I mean—the guard who knows Officer Al?"

"Yes, I am, but keep quiet about it."

"I wish the other guards were like you. Especially the night I came here when all those men beat us."

"I was part of that, but I only pretended to beat anyone. Whittaker hand selected guards for the beating rampage. Many were only too happy to comply."

"But not you."

"No. I can't strike a lady. What I witnessed was horrible."

"A gentleman, eh?"

"Me? I suppose so."

"Am I really being released today?"

"Well not really, in a couple of days you are. Now you keep eating so you have strength then."

He tried to trick me into breaking my hunger strike!

"Why does Suffrage scare you so?"

"It doesn't. I want to protect my country and teaching you Suffragettes a lesson is part of that."

"What about protecting our democracy?"

"Even though you're being released soon, the rules are still in effect and breaking any will subject you to discipline."

"Punishment."

"Yes. Go ahead and eat."

"I lost my appetite for bugs."

After he left, she whispered to the prisoner who now occupied the cell that Dora Lewis and Alice Cosu were in, before being transferred to the District jail, and Mary Nolan until she was released.

"Is it true?" whispered Kathryn.

"The release? It's true! November 27th or the day after, depending on which group we're in."

Kathryn tossed the food into the toilet and wadded up some toilet paper to toss over it. No ending the hunger strike today, not until she was actually released.

She flopped back onto the mat.

November 27th

Two people helped a depleted, just-released Kathryn Wolfe into a taxi, She had to focus to remain upright even with people on both sides helping her. She was groggy and when they got her into the back seat, one person sat on her left, the other on the right. A familiar voice came from the front seat.

"Kathryn," said Mary Dodd, "as soon as we got Genevieve's telegram, we took a train."

That brought Kathryn alert. "Mary, you all shouldn't have. You didn't leave Rose by herself!"

"No," said Rose who was sitting next to her.

"When we heard what happened," said Mary, "we had to come and wait for you to be released. We arrived five days ago. The prison administrators wouldn't let us visit you nor did they allow in letters from outside."

"Margarete wanted to be here," said George, "but she's on the picket line waiting for us to pick her up and go to the boarding house."

"What happened to Alice Paul?" asked Mary.

"They said she went on a hunger strike at the District jail and they sent her to the prison's psychiatric ward and force fed her."

"We went by the District jail first," said Mary, "George thought you might be there."

"We think Miss Paul is who we saw a couple of women carrying to a car," said George. She couldn't walk."

"She's much worse off than I am," said Kathryn, "and some of the hunger-strikers ended up in the hospital, but I'm all right and ready to go back to the picket line."

"No!" said the three of them in unison.

"We're taking you to the boarding house to recover," said Mary.

Kathryn was too exhausted to argue and she fell asleep on the way to pick up Margarete and to the boarding house.

Betty greeted them there.

They helped Kathryn through the door. "You look like you've been through a wringer," Betty said.

"She certainly has been," said Margarete. They held Kathryn's arm and led her to a sofa in the living room near the fireplace.

"It was all over the papers," said Betty. "There's been massive public outcry about the way you were all treated."

"We want to get you home, Kathryn," said Mary.

"I'll stay a couple more months," Kathryn mumbled.

Mary looked at Rose and George. "Then so will we."

Kathryn smiled and slid back on the sofa and closed her eyes.

DECMBER

As December rolled on, Kathryn started gaining her strength back and in the days leading up to Christmas she was able to shop a little at nearby stores. Later, she walked to and from the picket line a couple of times on snowy days. Like her fellow sentinels, she looked forward to an all-important day coming up in January.

CHAPTER FORTY-ONE

January 1918

Congress and DC

O n January 9, 1918, Kathryn celebrated with her fellow suffragists when President Wilson declared support for a Federal Woman Suffrage Amendment.

The next day, Kathryn and her friends along with a large number of other suffragists arrived early at the Capitol Building and packed the galleries of the cavernous House of Representatives chamber for the big Suffrage vote. Mary and Kathryn brought knitting as did many others. Claire brought lunch for several people.

Kathryn could feel the tension among her fellow suffragists as the congressmen and one congresswoman filtered in. Several men had to be helped to their seats, apparently sick, still showing up for the vote.

Mary leaned toward Kathryn. "This is exciting."

"It's been a long time coming," said Kathryn. "Elizabeth Cady Stanton foresaw this moment way back in 1868, and here we are."

As the representatives took their seats, Speaker of the House Champ Clark began the session. After preliminary business, he said:

"Chair wants to admonish the galleries that they are here by courtesy of the House. They are not here to help conduct the business of the House and it is against the rules for them to show any signs of assent or dissent by applause or otherwise.

"If I catch anybody violating that rule, I will clear the part of the gallery where they are."

Congressman John Raker approached the lectern to open the debate.

Without notice, Congressman Joseph Walsh asked, "Would it interfere seriously with your plans if you were to let Miss Rankin open the debate?"

"I yield my time to the gentlelady from Montana," Congressman Raker said.

Congresswoman Jeannette Rankin of Montana rose and started by mentioning American women leaders such as Susan B. Anthony, Elizabeth Cady Stanton, Clara Barton, and more. "All have asked the Government to permit women to serve more effectively the national welfare. During this time of war, may women be given the chance to serve their nation? As never before the Nation needs its women—needs the work of their hands and their hearts and their minds."

She spoke for her allotted time and concluded. "Can we afford to allow these men and women to doubt for a single instant the sincerity of our protestations of democracy? How shall we answer their challenge, gentlemen; how shall we explain to them the meaning of democracy if the same Congress that voted for war to make the world safe for democracy refuses to give this small measure of democracy to the women of our country?"

Sustained applause greeted her speech, which brought no reaction by the Speaker.

After some debate, Congressman Moon of Tennessee rose. "Mr. Speaker, before addressing myself briefly to the question, I ask unanimous consent to revise and extend the remarks I may make."

"The gentleman from Tennessee asks unanimous consent to revise and extend his remarks," said the Speaker. "Is there objection?"

"Mr. Speaker, for the present I shall object," Congressman Walsh of Massachusetts said.

"The gentleman from Massachusetts objects," said the Speaker.

"Mr. Speaker, I suspected as much," said Congressman Moon. "That is about all the gentleman from Massachusetts is capable of doing."

A quiet laughter rose from the galleries.

"Logically," Representative Moon began, "no man can deny that a woman is entitled to all the rights and privileges, including the right of Suffrage, that men enjoy; nor has man the moral right to determine whether it is best for women to exercise the right to vote or not. Women should be permitted to determine for themselves that which they think is best for them."

Mary and Kathryn nodded at each other and smiled.

However, Moon then went on to say that the voters should determine whether to make men and women equal and a Federal amendment would deprive the State of its legal right to determine its electorate. Finally, he said he couldn't support the Suffrage amendment because his constituents didn't.

"But you can do the right thing with your vote, anyway," muttered Kathryn.

After Congressman Moon finished his remarks, Speaker Clark said, "The gentleman from Kansas is recognized for ten minutes.

"Mr. Speaker," said Congressman Campbell, "the man who does not know that today witnesses the dawn of a new era in the progress of civilization of mankind fails to comprehend what is passing in the world. Old things are passing away and we are coming into new and greater things."

Kathryn and Mary leaned forward and smiled down at Margarete.

"He makes me proud to be a Kansan," said Kathryn.

Mary grasped Kathryn's elbow and smiled.

* * *

After more speeches, the representatives voted on a change to Article 1 of the Constitution having to do with electors. There were insufficient "yeas" to pass it.

When Speaker Clark announced the amendment didn't pass, Kathryn felt a sharp pain at the pit of her stomach.

"You really have to pay close attention," she said to Mary. "For a moment, I thought it was the Suffrage amendment that was rejected. Phew!"

After more speeches, and debate on other issues, the Representatives finally voted on the Nineteenth Amendment.

Kathryn and fellow suffragists leaned forward to hear the calls of "yeas" and "nays."

The "yeas" won and the chamber erupted in cheers.

Several Congressmen demanded a roll call.

During the roll call, Kathryn enjoyed reliving the moment as she and others listened to 274 "yeas" and 136 "nays" shouted with 17 not voting.

The resolution passed.

After closing business, the House adjourned. Kathryn, Mary, Rose, Genevieve, George, Margarete, and Claire stood and joined their fellow suffragists who spilled out from the galleries into the hall. One of the women present took a deep breath, looked up and broke into singing the Christian "Doxology."

"Praise God from whom all blessings flow. . ."

Mary joined her with her smooth voice followed by many. Their voices echoed throughout the marble halls.

When Kathryn and her companions descended the Capitol steps outside, Kathryn said, "It's tempting to think we're halfway there now."

"But we're not," said Margarete, "we need the Senate to pass it."

"I'm watching for that," said Claire. "There's no guarantee. Our job isn't finished. A triumph, yes, but we must keep up the pressure."

* * *

January 1918 in Washington, DC, was very cold, so whenever there was an occasional sunny, slightly mild day, Kathryn encouraged the others to go on walks with her. This day, they went to the National Mall.

"George said he'll meet us back at our boarding house later," said Mary as they reached the Mall area.

"It's fantastic," said Kathryn as they walked along an access road past the new Lincoln Memorial under construction. "When will it open to the public?"

"I've heard it's scheduled to open in 1922," said Claire. She pointed toward the massive structure.

"In there, they'll install an enormous statue of Lincoln so this magnificent building will have one appropriate resident. Sculptor Daniel Chester French designed it and the carvers in New York are set to finish it this year to send down for installation." She pointed to open area on the right. "There'll be a large reflecting pool there. Let's go to the Washington Monument."

They started to head to it about a mile east. When they reached the obelisk, Kathryn gazed up.

"I've been to the top," said Claire.

Mary went to the entrance. "Let's go in."

They entered and went to the stairway.

Kathryn regarded the stairway. "Ready to walk up?"

"Are you up to it?" asked Rose.

"I am. How about you?"

"I should be able to."

"Ready."

Kathryn had no problems when they started up by holding onto the handrail and when they reached the thirty-foot landing, she sat on the bench and stretched her leg.

Rose sat next to her. "Doing all right?" she asked, catching her breath.

"Just great. We'll make it."

The others waited for them to rest.

At the sixty-foot landing, everyone rested.

"We'll want to make it to the two hundred ten-foot landing not quite halfway up," said Claire.

"Why? What's there?" Kathryn asked.

"You'll all find out when we get there."

They made it to the one-hundred-foot landing and rested.

As they continued up, Kathryn again found an effective way to keep going by lifting her left leg at an angle with each step.

"Be careful, everyone," she said at one point, "I don't want to kick anybody."

"We should have brought one of those nice hecklers with us to walk along your left side," said Mary.

"Then I could trip him, watch him tumble down."

"Oh, dear," said Margarete, "I don't like this spiraling staircase anyway. Please no more mention of tumbling down. I don't like high up places. I didn't think this would bother me here inside."

"I'll keep quiet. Do you want to wait for us at the next landing?"

"I'll consider that, or perhaps I can take your arm, I'll stay along the wall as we go, and then we can help each other."

Kathryn agreed.

"Say, everyone," said Claire," did you know this wasn't the first Washington Monument? The first was built up on South Mountain in Maryland. Thirty feet tall from its base with a spectacular view of the Shenandoah Valley."

"No problem climbing that one, I'm sure," said Kathryn.

"I don't know if it has hand rails."

"That gives me an idea," said Kathryn.

"Do tell," said Mary.

"No. Not now."

Margarete and Kathryn walked up together as Claire and Rose followed.

Later.

"The two hundred ten-foot landing," said Claire. "We all made it. And now. . ."

Everyone paused to catch their breath while Claire went over to a section of the stone wall and pointed to an embedded Commemorative stone.

Kathryn, Mary, Rose, and Margarete crowded around it.

"It has the Kansas state seal," said Mary. "How fabulous!"

"So appropriate your state's motto, you all," said Claire. "Ad Astra per Aspera, To the stars through difficulties."

CHAPTER FORTY-TWO

March 1918

The Return

When Kathryn and the others stepped off the train at the Sycamore Falls depot, she took in a deep breath and smelled the familiar smells of Kansas March air that she couldn't name. But today the partly cloudy skies gave the town a welcoming feeling during this happy day for them after being away for so long.

A man approached from a ways down on the boarding platform.

"There's Mr. Markley," said Kathryn.

He came up to them. "I heard we had some visitors returning from afar," he said.

"So nice to be home," said Kathryn, shaking Markley's hand. "How are things here?"

"We're holding on. Theodore Miller is sick with influenza and he's home behind a closed door and not going out. The mayor has instructed anyone with the flu stay home and put a white scarf on the front doorknob to indicate virus within."

"Oh dear," said Rose. "How is he doing?"

"A nurse visited him and said he's fighting pneumonia, but I hear he's improving."

"I'm sorry to hear the flu has reached Kansas."

"No, the first reported case in the U.S. was in Haskell County in January. I know it's hitting our military boys really hard. I think Kansas is doing well, because people are avoiding the sick and practicing good hygiene. We haven't been hit hard in Sycamore Falls. Anyone who has to go near the sick is wearing a mask and there are limited large gatherings."

"I'm glad about that," said Kathryn.

He nodded and said, "But you've all got good news, don't you?"

Rose put her arm around Kathryn.

"You've heard about the House passing the amendment?" Kathryn said.

"We have," he said. "It's caused excitement all over town. Not everyone is happy about it, but many are."

"Now, if only the Senate would get to work on it. I heard they won't bring it up until October."

"It's time to write to Senators Thompson and Curtis. And, say, my hill is open whenever you want to go trailing."

"I would love that after settling in," said Kathryn. She looked at the others. "What about you all?"

All nodded.

Kathryn, Rose, and Mary headed to Main Street. "Ah, so peaceful," said Kathryn. "Nothing like being away for almost a year to see one's town as an outsider sees it."

"How does it look, Kathryn?" said George.

"It looks nice. It's a nice town. Slower than I'm used to now, you think, Margarete?"

"It's refreshing. Soothing. After what you went through in that awful prison, we can relax and not fear for your safety."

"Mary," after I check in at home, I should go by the shop."

"It's locked up tight and I organized everything before I left."

"Thank you!"

Margarete and George headed on to their homes and Rose, Mary, and Kathryn went to Kathryn's house. A stack of mail waited for Kathryn including the latest issue of *The Suffragist*. They went in and she tossed the mail on a table. "Let's see," she said, pulling the newsletter out. "Say, look! A Federal Appeals Court declared our arrests and imprisonment were unconstitutional."

"Well, of course," said the others.

"You shouldn't have had to endure that," said Margarete.

Kathryn flopped onto the sofa and sighed.

A knock at the door.

"Anne and Anna" said Kathryn. "Come in!"

"We heard about your imprisonment, Kathryn," said Anne.

"Well, what's new around town?" said Kathryn.

"Anna and I are active in the local Suffrage Movement. We've been holding meetings, sales, and whatever we can do to keep the issue active. Violette has been joining us."

"You would have been proud of Congressman Campbell," said Mary. "His speech was very persuasive and to the point."

"Well? What else?" said Kathryn. "Any other news? About anyone in particular?"

"News, but it's not good news," said Anna.

"John?" said Rose. "What's he done? Is he trying to steer people away from Suffrage?"

"We didn't want to send a telegram to Washington about it," said Anne. She held back tears. "I'm so sorry to tell you, Rose, but John's dead."

"Oh!" Rose gasped. She brought her hands to her face and cried softly. "Oh, what happened! Was it influenza?"

"No," said Anna, "but he was very sick."

"He died of syphilis," said Anne.

"How terrible!" said Rose.

"But—" said Kathryn, "There are effective treatments for it now."

"Doc Hall said John didn't see him for treatment. He thought John didn't want it to get around so he pushed it aside, maybe didn't realize what it could do to him."

Everyone gathered around Rose to console her.

"I'll be all right," Rose said. "as long as I have you all as friends."

CHAPTER FORTY-THREE

April 1918

Before and After

On a sunny late April day, Kathryn and some of her friends walked to the park.

"I'm so glad it cleared up," Kathryn said. She put her hand on Rose's shoulder.

"Nice weather helps," said Rose. She turned to the others. "Thank all of you for coming here with me today." She gestured to the far bench. "That is my special place, my refuge. I spent a lot of sad times there, but today I want to go there first."

The group complied and they walked to the bench.

"This is where Mary and I first met you, Rose," said Kathryn.

"It sure is," said Rose. "I was upset that day because John and I had had a fight. And—"

"Oh, Rose!" said Anna, "I still feel bad about what happened that day."

"Remember, I said to think nothing of it, Anna." Rose stepped over to her. "And he cheated on *you* with

Anne!" Rose broke into uncontrollable laughter which started the rest.

Margarete calmed and said with a chuckle, "We might get in trouble for disturbing the peace."

"At least we're not in DC where we'd be tortured and sentenced to life," said Kathryn.

"I do miss Claire," said Margarete.

"I do, too," said Kathryn. "And Genevieve and Roscoe were so nice. I miss them, too. I wonder if we'll ever them again. DC is such a long way away. Well, never mind that; today is for Rose, so let's go."

They all locked arms and bounced through the park toward the entrance. George headed on with Margarete, Anna, and Rose to get his car.

Kathryn and Mary went to the bookshop to wait for George to bring his car. They went in and the smell of books greeted them.

"Ahhh, the aroma of literature," said Kathryn. "Has it ever smelled so sweet! And, Mary, look what you've done here this week! It never looked better. What a dear you are."

A car horn sounded out front.

"George already!" said Mary.

They went out and found Rose, Anna and Margarete already piled in the back seat. Anna opened the door. "Room for one more!" They laughed while Mary climbed in and sat across their laps amid a chorus of giggles.

"Up front, Kathryn," said Margarete, laughing so hard she almost cried. "You're not invited to this party back here."

Kathryn climbed onto the front seat and closed the door. She turned around to the commotion in the back seat. "Now ladies, be careful and don't distract George. We don't want to wind up as permanent residents where we're going."

"Well," said George, "you haven't seen some of my students. I think I can handle a car full of adults."

"Adults?" said Kathryn, laughing.

"We're sorry, Rose," said Margarete. "We're laughing when we should be somber."

Rose laughed. "It's all right. I am fine."

They drove north then east to the edge of town and pulled in and parked.

Anna led Rose to a relatively fresh grave.

Rose started to cry. "Oh, John, you could have had such a great life. "Why, why, why?" She looked like she wanted to stomp on the just-sprouting grass.

Kathryn took Rose's hand and led her whimpering from the grave.

CHAPTER FORTY-FOUR

July 1918

Canvass

Violette Stephens often took walks on Sunday afternoons when the weather was nice. On an unseasonably cool Sunday in early July, she walked down Main Street past the hotel where she veered out around the remodeling construction of the hotel on Third and Main. She looked forward to the reopen in the 1920s.

That great hotel might attract people to visit and perhaps there'd be a new era in Sycamore Falls.

She started thinking.

Maybe sometime in that next decade there will be a new era for women. Who knows when? Other states have passed Women's Suffrage since Kansas did in 1912, but it's been slow-going.

Have I done all I can for the Movement? Even George Fielding is doing a lot and taking criticism and went to Washington. Twice! And Mary, Margarete, and poor Rose. Also, Kathryn enduring torture in prison. But what have I done? Oh, boy, what should I do?

She stopped at Weber's Grocery, picked up sandwich fixings and continued down Main Street to the park. Under a shady tree, she had a sandwich. As she relaxed in the afternoon peace and gazed around the park, she came up with an idea. This afternoon was a good time to get to it. She checked her small handbag for a pencil and piece of paper. Working in a school, she always carried those with her. She had what she needed.

She stood and stretched. It was still plenty early, approaching two o'clock so she left the park and walked up Main Street past Prairie Hills Feed Store to First Street and turned right. She summoned her bravery and decided she would start with the first house on the right. It was a bungalow style with a nice porch and looked recently painted. She went up the steps and knocked on the door. She didn't notice the can of paint that sat to the side until just then.

A man opened the door and looked at the porch floor.

"Hm," he said with a scowl, "I guess it's dry enough. Do you know what you almost did, woman?"

"I'm sorry, I didn't realize it was that fresh."

"Then what do you need? The lady of the house is out. Tell me what you want and I'll pass it along to her."

"Will she be home later?"

"I don't know. She's at one of those damned women's club meetings."

"All right. Thank you." Violette turned and left with him grumbling as she stepped onto the front walk.

Whew. Now she knew to pay closer attention to things. Didn't people usually put out a "wet paint" sign?

She walked to the next house, another bungalow. No mistaking that paint for wet. Soon it would need a coat. She walked up to the front door and knocked.

A middle-aged woman answered and Violette felt relieved. "Yes?" the woman said.

"Hello, I'm Violette."

"Yes, I think I've seen you before at the high school."

"That's right! Well, I just stopped by to ask you to consider writing to Senators Thompson and Curtis and encourage them to support women's right to vote."

"Now, Violette, I appreciate your opinion on that, but won't that drive a wedge between men and women and where's our femininity if we get involved in voting?"

"We can keep it. It allows us to have a say when choosing our leaders."

"Next thing you know, women will be running for things that are better left to men," the woman said.

Violette wanted to remind her that women had already been elected to mayoral offices in several Kansas towns.

"Well," said Violette, "thank you for your time." The woman went back in and quickly closed the door.

Violette skipped down to the sidewalk and wrote a couple of notes on the paper as she walked along the sidewalk. She caught a glimpse of the woman in her backyard talking to her neighbor so she continued past the neighbor's house and when she reached the corner, she crossed the street and went to the large foursquare-style house. A man and woman perhaps in their fifties sat on a porch swing.

"Hello, there," said both.

"Good afternoon," said Violette. "May I come up?"

"Of course," said the man.

She went up and joined them. "Hello, I'm Violette. Would you consider writing to Senators Thompson and Curtis and encourage them to support the amendment granting women the right to vote?"

"I will," said the woman.

"Ohh, I might consider it," said the man.

The woman slapped his leg. "Of course you will."

"I'll do it. I wasn't in favor of it at first, you know, but we have it in Kansas and now it should be law at the Federal level."

"Do you need their addresses?" said Violette, offering since she didn't have them with her.

"I think we can find them," he said.

"The library can help us if we need them," the woman said.

"Thank you both very much," said Violette as she started to leave.

"Bye now and good luck," the man said.

Violette continued along that side of First Street. The next house, no one was home. At the house after that, the man who answered wasn't interested in talking. At a house farther down the block, an older woman was working in her flower bed out front. She was interested in hearing about the amendment and said she'd write. Violette made a note and promised to bring the addresses by.

A couple of blocks later, Violette headed north and stopped at more houses. She was establishing an average of agreeable vs. not and recorded her results. After zigzagging around some streets, she ran into Rose.

They exchanged greetings and Violette told her what she was doing. "Would you like to join me?"

Rose looked at her locket watch. "I'd love to. I was headed to the park, but this sounds good."

"I just came from the park," said Violette, "and was relaxing under a tree when I decided to do this. The park's a good place to think."

"It sure is. I go to my special place to think and relax when I'm having a bad day."

"You've had so much sadness, I admire your resilience."

"Thank you. Friends help," said Rose. "I didn't have many friends around town when John and I were together."

"I was so sorry to hear about John, but I hated the way he treated you."

"He often yelled about women's vote. I never understood why it brought out such violence in him—and in others, too, what with how Kathryn was treated in prison just for holding up a sign outside the White House."

"It's awful and very puzzling," said Violette. "I realized I haven't done enough to help the Movement, so by walking around town to knock on doors and talk to anyone who'll listen about why Suffrage is crucial for women and for men, I think I'm doing some good."

"Look." She pulled out the paper showing Rose the results.

"That is wonderful," said Rose. "Your efforts are paying off."

"Let's head on."

They went to another house, onto the porch and knocked. They smiled at the man who opened the door.

He smiled back. "What can I do for you ladies?"

"We have a question," said Rose.

He leaned forward.

"The senate will vote on an amendment for granting women's right to vote. Would you consider writing to our U.S. Senators to encourage them to support the amendment?"

"The Nineteenth Amendment? Didn't Congress already pass it a few months ago?"

"The House passed it in January and the Senate will consider it this session," said Violette.

"Then I should write to them. Thank you both for the reminder. My fiancée also supports Suffrage. I'll tell her."

When they reached the sidewalk, Rose said, "Well, some are receptive and others aren't. I suggest a strategy. Since some are against Suffrage, they might see our visit as a reminder to write to our senators and ask them to vote *against* the amendment."

"I think I know what you're going to suggest," said Violette.

"What then?"

"Start by asking what they think about it and encourage them to write if they show they're for it, otherwise don't mention writing to senators."

"Oh, you're as devious as I am, you little sneak, you."

"I'll try to live up to your expectations."

They knocked on the front door of the next house and a young woman answered.

"Hello," said Rose, "what is your opinion about the Nineteenth Amendment that the Senate will vote on this fall?"

"Oh! I'm all for it. I have my fingers crossed."

"So do we," said Violette. "Would you consider writing to Senators Thompson and Curtis and encourage them to support the Amendment?"

I will. I write to them about a lot of things."

They thanked her and went on to the next block. A man sat on the ground next to the front walk with a tray of mortar and a trowel smoothing out a repair he made to the sidewalk.

As they walked toward him, Violette said loud enough for him to hear: "Oh, he's busy, let's not bother him."

The man looked up. "It's all right, ladies. What's on your mind?"

"The upcoming Senate vote on the Amendment to allow women to vote."

The man looked up toward the porch where a woman stood holding a baby. "Well, he said, "I think it's about time."

"Will you write to Senators Thompson and Curtis and encourage them to support the amendment?"

"I sure will."

They thanked him and returned to the sidewalk. "Did you see the smirk on the woman's face?" whispered Rose. They continued on a little ways and heard the man talking to her. Rose stopped over behind the wide trunk of a tree while Violette walked on and wrote on her paper. After a short while, Violette stopped and Rose joined her.

"What did you hear? asked Violette.

"He was lying," said Rose. "He told the woman that he got rid of us."

"Oh, my. He's as devious as we are."

"But we're not lying. Devious, but we're not lying."

"We can just continue on as we have."

After crossing the street, they passed by a side yard where children were throwing a baseball around. A boy stopped and stared at Violette.

"Is your mother or father home?" Violette asked the boy.

"He turned to a girl. "Go get Mom!"

"No!" said the girl.

The boy tossed the ball to another and ran inside then emerged pulling his mother by her arm out toward the sidewalk.

The mother walked up to Violette.

"Well, hello, Mrs. Stephens," she said, then glanced at Rose.

"Oh, pardon me," said Violette, "this is Rose Shane."

"Pleased to meet you, Rose. I heard about your ordeal. I'm so sorry. Say, why don't you two come in for coffee? I just made a pot."

Violette looked at Rose who nodded.

On the way in, the woman turned to Rose. "Please excuse my rudeness, I am Loraine Howell."

"I'm sorry I didn't introduce you," said Violette.

Inside, they admired Loraine's paintings and wall hangings adorning the walls.

"Please sit," said Loraine. She retrieved a coffee pot and cups from the kitchen and handed the cups to Rose and Violette.

"I think I know why you're in the neighborhood," said Loraine. "Are you collecting donations for the cause?"

"Well," said Rose, "we're looking for support, yes. Would you consider writing to Senators Thompson and Curtis and encourage them to support the Amendment?"

"I can do more than that," Loraine said, standing up. She went into another room and returned with a small box, sat and opened it. "My crochet hooks." From beneath the hooks, she pulled out a stack of bills. "I have a hundred twenty-two dollars here. Mr. Howell wouldn't want me donating to the Kansas Equal Suffrage Association. I've been stashing this away for some time for anything special."

"Mrs. Howell," said Rose, "we do appreciate your generosity, but we're not collecting donations. We're asking people to write to our U.S. Senators to vote "yea" on the Nineteenth Amendment granting women the right to vote across the country."

"My mistake! I'm behind the times. Yes, of course I'll write to them. When is the vote?"

"We believe it'll be this fall," said Violette.

Rose cleared her throat. "Well, thank you for your hospitality, Mrs. Howell. We have more rounds to make."

Violette stood and thanked Loraine as well.

After a while, Rose decided she needed a rest and excused herself to go to the park.

"That's all right," said Violette. "If you'd like company, I'll join you, but if you prefer to be alone, that's fine, too."

"Thank you. I am going to my special place."

"Of course. I'll leave you to that then. I think we had a successful afternoon. I appreciate you joining me."

They split and Violette reviewed her results as she walked. Not bad. A fair number said they'd write to encourage support. She walked along Fifth Street toward downtown and decided to head home while it was still daylight.

A half block from Main Street, she glanced up when two men approached.

She stepped aside when they blocked her way. "You're one of them, aren't you?" said one of the men.

"She's one," said the other. He took hold of her arm. The other grabbed the other arm and they dragged her into the alley.

"Why do you women have to go causing trouble around town like you're doing!" shouted the first. He held her arms behind her back and the other struck her in the face.

She screamed. "Leave me alone!"

An older man across the street made his way over to them.

"Leave her alone! You hit a lady!" He grabbed one of the men.

"That ain't no lady," the man said. He pushed the older man to the pavement.

"That's your first lesson, school secretary," the first man said. He threw her to the ground. "Come on," he said to the other and they ran down the alley.

"Cowards!" yelled the older man to the laughter of the running men.

Violette stood and brushed off her jacket. She offered her hand to the fallen man and helped him up. "Oh, thank you, sir," she said while catching her breath. "Are you all right?"

"I am fine, but you're going to have quite a shiner there," he said, pointing to her eye.

"Those hateful men," she said.

* * *

Several days later during the noon hour at Main Street Bookshop, Kathryn and Mary prepared to arrange some new titles.

The bell jingled and Violette entered.

"Your eye looks awful," said Mary.

"You poor thing," said Kathryn. "Did you see Doc Hall for it?"

"No, I'll be all right."

The door jingled and Fred Markley entered with a newspaper tucked under his arm. He stood back politely as the others finished their conversation.

"Well! I wouldn't have believed it!" he boomed as he opened the paper.

"Hello, Mr. Markley," said Violette, echoed by the others.

"Ladies. Mrs. Stephens, be assured the good people in town won't stand for this." He held the paper up. "Look what this editorial in the *Prospect* says about that attack."

"As Kansas passed Women's Suffrage in 1912, many here already support the Federal Amendment and we believe this unfortunate incident is inspiring our citizens to write to our Senators, given the number of letters *The Sycamore Falls Weekly Prospect* has received in support of Mrs. Stephens' and Mrs. Shane's efforts."

"There was a witness, wasn't there?" said Fred.

"I believe it was Mr. Crow who came to my aid," said Violette. "I think he got hurt. I hope he's all right."

"He's fine. He's a tough old guy and he comes by the ranch often. And remember you're all welcome to traipse up that hill whenever you like. Take care of yourself, Mrs. Stephens."

"I want to get up there," said Kathryn, "but I think I'll wait until the cooler weather."

"Anytime."

CHAPTER FORTY-FIVE

September 1918

Main Street Bookshop

Kathryn worked on some pending tasks in the bookshop most of the morning after opening up the shop. Mary would be in for the afternoon. As she sorted through the mail again, she kept looking through the most recent issue of *The Suffragist*, but no matter how many times she did, that wasn't going to cause any new articles to appear about the Senate taking up the Amendment for a vote.

Mary came in and helped with getting ready for the week.

Later in the afternoon, the bell jingled and a young man stepped in. "Telegram for Kathryn Wolfe."

Kathryn stepped over and gave him a nickel.

"Thank you!" he said, handing the envelope to her then he skipped out the door.

Kathryn opened the telegram.

WASHINGTON, DC SEP 30, 1918
KATHRYN WOLFE
MAIN STREET BOOKSHOP SYCAMORE
FALLS KANSAS

PRESIDENT WILSON DELIVERED SPEECH
TO SENATE.
REMINDED THEM NATION IS AT WAR.
COULD NOT BE FOUGHT
WITHOUT SERVICES OF WOMEN.
IMPLORED SENATORS TO PASS THE
AMENDMENT TOMORROW.

WE HOPE HIS APPEAL TO THE SENATE IS
NOT TOO LATE

WILL SEND TELEGRAM TOMORROW
AFTER VOTE.
BE WELL
CLAIRE

"Mary, would you like to read it? I'm so anxious, I don't think I'll sleep tonight."

Mary read the message. Her expression brightened. "I won't sleep, either!"

* * *

Late that night, Kathryn tossed in bed and couldn't relax her mind so she could drift to sleep. She got up and pulled on her robe, went downstairs.

Rose was next to the fireplace on a cushy chair with a throw blanket over her lap sipping warm cocoa as a small lamp cast dim light. "I took it upon myself to make some cocoa," she said. There's plenty in the kitchen next to the stove."

"May I join you?" said Kathryn as she went to get a cup. She returned with a plate of oatmeal cookies and set them on the table between their chairs.

"Please do."

"I can't sleep, either," said Kathryn.

"I think our senators will vote yes," said Rose, "but those from some other states, I am more concerned."

"I think you're right about Thompson and Curtis. If there had been any question, I bet your efforts with Violette helped make a difference.

"I hope so."

"Wilson has a party majority in the Senate. Hopefully, they'll fall in line with his plea."

They sat up for hours before finally going to bed.

* * *

Kathryn spent the next day fidgeting as she worked.

"Please relax," said Mary several times. "Think how Alice Paul and Lucy Burns feel right now."

"I can't relax. We're just hours or minutes away from finding out if a half century of Suffrage campaigning will be decided in our favor. I can't concentrate on anything."

Later in the day, the telegram arrived.

Kathryn handed the envelope to Mary, her hands shaking.

WASHINGTON, DC OCT 1, 1918
KATHRYN WOLFE
MAIN STREET BOOKSHOP SYCAMORE FALLS KANSAS

SAD TO REPORT THE 65TH CONGRESS WILL LIKELY END

WITHOUT PASSING SUFFRAGE. SENATE REJECTED
AMENDMENT TODAY. FAILED BY TWO VOTES.
SEN ANDRIEUS JONES PROMISED TO CALL ANOTHER
VOTE BEFORE SESSION ENDS IN MARCH 1919.

THE CAMPAIGN CONTINUES.

BE WELL
- CLAIRE

CHAPTER FORTY-SIX

May 1919

Try Again

After the President's party lost control of the Senate in the November 1918 election, March 1919 came and went without another vote on the Nineteenth Amendment.

On Wednesday, May 21, 1919, around the noon hour, Violette and Rose entered the bookshop.

"Did you know there's a House vote today?" said Violette.

"I'm expecting a telegram from Claire later," said Kathryn. "I need to take a walk to relax."

"Yes, let's go," said Mary. "We can close up the shop. Rose and Violette, will you join us?"

Violette encouraged the three of them to go. "I'll stay. I could spend hours browsing in your bookshop and I'll watch for Claire's telegram."

Violette went to the bookshelves. They thanked her and stepped out to the sidewalk.

"Where to?" asked Mary.

Kathryn gestured toward the north then noticed Theodore Miller approaching from there.

"No, let's cross the street and head south," she said.

As they turned to cross, Miller shouted: "Ladies!"

"Never mind—" said Kathryn.

They stayed and waited for him.

"Hello, Mr. Miller," said Kathryn.

"Have you heard the news?" he said.

"Yes, there's a House vote today on the Suffrage Amendment," said Mary.

"They've adjourned," he said. "Woman Suffrage passed 304 to 90. I'm sure you're all happy to hear that."

"That's excellent news, Mr. Miller!" said Kathryn.

When Miller looked away for a moment, Kathryn whispered: "I would have been happier to hear it from Claire."

Mary snickered quietly.

"Rose," Miller said, "you might like to meet my nephew who'll be in town in a couple of weeks."

"Thank you, no," said Rose. "It's too soon."

"Well," Miller said, tipping his hat, "if you ladies will excuse me, I'll take my leave." He went back the way he came.

"How about it, Rose?" said Kathryn, tapping her shoulder, chuckling.

"I'm busy. I hope to be celebrating the Senate vote in a couple of weeks. I won't need distractions."

"There's always time later if you decide that's for you," said Mary.

"I don't want to worry about that. Anticipating the Senate vote and ratification will be enough to keep me busy."

"Me, too," echoed the others.

CHAPTER FORTY-SEVEN

June 1919

Goal

Two weeks later on June 4th, Kathryn and Mary were in tears as they closed the shop in the evening after the news arrived and they went out onto the sidewalk. They turned north and started walking.

"It really happened! We have an Amendment!" said Mary. "I never thought we'd see this day!"

Kathryn laughed and cried at the same time "I can't believe it, either!"

As they walked, they heard shouts from behind.

"Kathryn! Mary! Wait!"

Kathryn and Mary turned around and saw Margarete, Rose, and George running toward them. Violette and Anna ran from across the street to join them.

The group reached Kathryn and Mary.

"Kathryn, Mary, look! Go back this way!" Margarete gestured south. Shop owners lined the sidewalks in front of their stores.

"What's all that?" asked Kathryn.

"Spur of the moment when the news hit. People poured out onto the sidewalks."

Kathryn and friends walked south from the bookshop, past other businesses, then reached Markley's Furniture Company. Fred stood out front, clapping when they passed by. Women and men shopkeepers along the block stood clapping with more applause across the street, two people in front of Ranchers Bank, and most business owners along that side of the street.

Mayor MacGregor stood in the intersection of Third Street and Main with a cop who cleared Main Street of traffic and the mayor gestured to Kathryn's group to come out to the middle of the street.

"Main Street is yours!" he said.

The applause grew louder as they continued.

After making their way along several blocks to the cheers of their friends and neighbors, they reached the city park.

Kathryn separated Rose from the others and led her to her special place.

Rose was hesitant. "But why here?"

Kathryn took her by the shoulders. "This is your *happy place* now!"

Rose broke down. The others reached them along with other townspeople, then everyone walked back onto Main Street together.

A couple of hours later, Kathryn settled onto a chair in her living room. Rose relaxed as well.

"I wish Mary could have stayed," said Rose.

"I think she's doing the same as we are at her place."

"We finally did it, Kathryn."

"And now we wait for the states to ratify and I know how I'll commemorate those."

"Oh?"
"But I'm too tired now to think about it."
Both dozed in their chairs.

CHAPTER FORTY-EIGHT

June 1919 – August 1920

Ratification

On June 10, 1919, Kathryn entered the ornate courthouse's large lobby with Mary, Rose, and Margarete.

"Are you wondering why I brought you here?" she asked. "Because of Michigan and Wisconsin ratifying today! Thirty-six states to ratify the Amendment." She gestured over to the wide stairway. There are thirty-five steps to the top, one less than the number of states that need to ratify. For each state that ratifies, I'll walk from the bottom up the number of steps of how many have ratified so far. That is, when the eighth state ratifies, I'll walk up eight steps from the bottom. When the ninth state ratifies, I'll start at the bottom again and walk up nine steps.

"She went across the lobby to the stairs and took the first step with her right foot without holding on to the handrail.

"Kathryn, be careful," said Margarete.

"I tried it yesterday. I'll grab the handrail if I need to."

For the second step, she swung her left foot out, planted it on the step, felt a bit off balance, but recovered and took the handrail.

"For Michigan and Wisconsin," she said.

"You can do it," said Mary.

"It's different from trailing because of the low height of each step."

* * *

On June 16th, Kathryn's friends joined her in the courthouse.

She went to the stairway and spoke loud enough to echo throughout: "Today is for New York, Ohio, and our great state of Kansas!"

Her friends applauded. She walked up five steps for the five states ratifying so far without holding on to the handrail. On the fifth step, she wobbled a bit, but managed to remain stable and took hold of the handrail.

* * *

On June 17th, the group in the lobby grew to a dozen.

"This is for Illinois which finalized its ratification today!" Kathryn said, adding one step to her ascent.

* * *

On June 24th, a larger group in the lobby waited.

"For Pennsylvania!" She added another step and walked up without the handrail, feeling more stable, having improved her technique.

July 1, 1920

By July 1, 1920, Massachusetts and thirty-four states had ratified the Amendment. Kathryn accumulated that many more steps which put her up on the top step to cheers from below. She addressed the crowd, which included reporters and photographers from *The Sycamore Falls Weekly Prospect* and *The Wichita Falcon*.

"We need one more state to ratify!" she shouted.

"When that happens, we'll all cheer!" shouted a reporter up from the lobby.

"On that day, I'll get to the top!" she shouted back.

A Month and a half later, Kathryn got the telegram.

WASHINGTON, DC AUGUST 18, 1920
KATHRYN WOLFE
   MAIN STREET BOOKSHOP SYCAMORE FALLS KANSAS

TENNESSEE RATIFIES! THANKS TO TENNESSEE STATE SEN BURNS
   WAITING ON U.S. SECRETARY OF STATE TO SIGN IT INTO LAW.
   WOMEN VOTE!

.

      CONGRATULATIONS!
      CLAIRE

CHAPTER FORTY-NINE

August 26 & 27, 1920

Women Vote!

After a failed attempt in Tennessee to introduce a motion to reconsider, U.S. Secretary of State Bainbridge Colby signed the Nineteenth Amendment into law on August 26, 1920.

* * *

The next morning, in the early hours before the day's heat, George parked the car on West Hill Road along a curve where the wooden pole fence began.

"Kathryn," he said, "if you'd like to go on to the trail, we'll meet you at the base of the hill."

"Thank you," she said.

She climbed out of the Model T, stretched her leg, and started walking along the gravel road. She loved the leafy smells and the cooling of the foliage above. The gravel road stretched on. When she reached the break in the fence, she stepped into the woods. A ways in, she stopped along the trail where she gazed around at the trees and felt the quiet of early morning. Soothing but time to head on. She continued to where the trail opened onto the prairie. The summer insects sang in the first glimmers of early morning light as she went through the tallgrass to the covered wagon ruin. Sugar Loaf towered above still waiting for her with its glowing yellow summit high enough to catch the sunrise.

She found a clear spot to sit and wait for her friends until movement from the woods trail signaled their arrival onto the grassland. She stood when George, Mary, and Rose arrived.

"Ready, Kathryn?" said Mary.

"Let's climb this hill," said Kathryn.

They started along the trail and Kathryn repeated her leg swing that worked well.

The ascent to the Promontory went well. Kathryn and Rose sat and marveled at the sunrise which cast long shadows, exaggerating the hills and valleys.

Rose sighed. "Like you said once, Kathryn, 'I never tire of this view'."

"I never do."

Nor do I," said Mary.

"Nor I," said George.

They all stood and started along the upper trail. Kathryn continued her leg technique.

"I'm glad you found that way of swinging your leg out that works," said Mary as she took her arm.

"It took a lot of work, but the freedom to pick trails that are good for me will be worth it."

After swishing for a while through shoulder-high tallgrass on the upper trail, they reached the ring of boulders near the hilltop.

George and Mary pulled Kathryn over the rocks and Kathryn's feet landed where they had never before been. After they helped Rose over, she and Kathryn clasped hands and easily walked up the rest of the way to the summit of Sugar Loaf.

When they reached the top, Kathryn caught her breath and gazed out at the rolling hillscape. She saw motion in the corner of her eye as Margarete emerged with Claire and Genevieve onto the hilltop.

Kathryn fell to her knees.

Claire came over and knelt next to her. "We heard so much about this Sugar Loaf hill of yours that we had to take a train out here right after Tennessee ratified. So nice of Margarete to pick us up."

"And we missed you," said Genevieve.

Kathryn stood as Margarete pulled champagne glasses and a bottle of ginger ale from her bag and Kathryn's camera which Genevieve took.

Kathryn held up her glass and beckoned her friends to pose with her as everyone's hair floated free on the hilltop breeze.

ABOUT THE AUTHOR

Photo credit: Nancy Reynolds

Eric T. Reynolds was born in the Flint Hills town, Eureka, Kansas, has also lived elsewhere in Kansas, and on the US East Coast. His fiction has appeared in the magazines *Mythic Circle*, *Galaxy's Edge*, in *Sci Phi Journal*, and in several indie press publications, and he had several non-fiction science articles published in an encyclopedia about the history of space exploration. *The Road to Sugar Loaf* is his second novel. His first, *The Artifacts*, was released in 2019 to critical acclaim. Contact him at erictreynolds@gmail.com and on Facebook as Eric T. Reynolds.